The
Falling Leaf

The
Falling Leaf

AAVINASH CHALIHA

Woven Words Publishers OPC Pvt. Ltd.

Registered Office:

Vill: Raipur, P.O: Raipur Paschimbar,

Dist: Purba Midnapore, Pin: 721401,

West Bengal, India.

www.wovenwordspublishers.in

Email: editor@wovenwordspublishers.in

First published by Woven Words Publishers OPC Pvt. Ltd., 2018

Copyright© Aavinash Chaliha, 2018

NOVELLA

IMPRINT: WOVEN WORDS

ISBN 13: 978-93-86897-21-3

ISBN 10: 9386897210

Price: $10/₹ 300

Printed and bound in India

ACKNOWLEDGEMENTS

I would like to thank the people around me whose moral support has greatly aided me in completing this novel. I would like to thank my family for being my pillar of strength. Also, my friends who have stood by me during trying times. I would like to thank Puspita Das Barabara, Pritisha Borthakur and Chandrani Sinha who stood by me when I needed them the most; without their help it would have been greatly difficult for me to complete my book.

A word of thanks to Wikipedia for being my guide and helping with the details of some of the places mentioned in this book.

Last but not the least, I would like to extend my gratitude to Mosiur Rehman and Woven Words Publishers OPC Pvt. Ltd. for giving me the opportunity to express my creativity in print, and giving me my publishing break.

CHAPTER-1

The biting chill of Delhi in the first days of January is rather infamous. No matter how many layers of clothing a person wears to ward it off, it somehow manages to seep into the bones to make its presence felt. A warm bed is the most welcome refuge in winter evenings in Delhi. After a hard day at work, Abhishek should have headed straight to his Paying Guest accommodation, relaxing on a warm bed under the blanket. Instead, in that cold evening he stood at the exit of the Vishwavidyalaya metro station, tired and exhausted, trying to get a rickshaw to the Vijay Nagar double storey. He checked his watch; it was ten minutes past seven.

The chill in the air was getting worse every passing minute and the grey pullover and blazer he wore provided him with little comfort. His ears were numb from the cold and he was frantically rubbing both his palms together and blowing his warm breath in between but with little effect. His cotton trousers failed miserably in protecting him from the cold and he could feel his knees start to tremble. In a desperate attempt to keep himself warm he frequently changed his stance, shifting his weight from his right foot to his left and vice versa. He was not sure of the benefits but the exercise distracted his mind from the weather. Abhishek did not like the cold winter of Delhi, but he had learnt to co-exist.

In spite of all that, Abhishek was in a happy mood. It was Friday and he was on his way to Amit's place in the evening. It was a chance encounter, on the New Year's Eve, which made him collide into his former classmate; a person whom he had not met for years.

***

It was around seven in the evening during the New Year's Eve. Abhishek was standing outside a wine shop in Kingsway Camp, waiting for his chance to go to the counter and get his hands on a bottle of whiskey. He usually doesn't drink too much but on special occasions he liked to indulge a bit.

Kingsway Camp, officially known as Guru Teg Bahadur Nagar, in north Delhi is the favoured address for thousands of outstation students coming to the city for higher studies. Situated within a walking distance of Delhi University's north campus, the rented apartments in Kingsway camp sees an influx of people from all over the country. Originally known as Kingsway, the small locality has a brief yet pivotal role in the archives of Indian history. It was home to the Coronation Park where the foundation of the new capital of British India in New Delhi was laid down by King George during his visit to the city. Yet it had also witnessed troubled times. Post the partition of India, Kingsway Camp was home to over 300,000 refugees coming in from Pakistan. Over the years, the people who were displaced from their roots have settled there.

Many decades have passed since and today Kingsway Camp bears a fresh and youthful vibrancy courtesy the close proximity of Delhi University. While the teeming young crowd of students gives the area a youthful buzz it also brings forth its share of dilemma. On festive occasions the restaurants, eateries and the wine shops are too crowded to even set foot. Jostling for space, pick pocketing and even fights are a common occurrence.

On the New Year's Eve, standing in front of the wine shop Abhishek was getting a sense of déjà vu seeing the unruly crowd fighting each other trying to reach the counter for a bottle of liquor. Some took more than five and it was justified for that one day. For just that day, there was no social discrimination as the rich, poor, young and old, shoved and pushed each other to reach the counter first. It was 31st December and everyone knew about the significance of the date; the crowd had assembled in the afternoon itself. Abhishek came as early as he could, but even seven in the evening seemed like a peak shopping hour. All the jostling, shouting and swearing made Abhishek feel uneasy. Being socially inhibitive, he never liked crowds in the first place; they were too loud and boisterous and created trouble. He did not know if there was any specific word to describe his condition, but the crowd made him uneasy; it brought back his disturbing memories; memories which he tried to forget but in vain. He grabbed his wallet carefully in an attempt to keep it safe from pick-pockets.

Suddenly he saw a figure that looked oddly familiar, he was not too sure though. He had only seen the back of the head and unless the fellow turned his face Abhishek couldn't confirm if he was the same guy who he thought he was. Just then the person turned around and Abhishek was pleasantly surprised. The person standing in front of him was Amit Baishya. Amit, affectionately called *Ami* during his school days, was Abhishek's former class mate in St. Patrick Boys School in Guwahati from where they both completed their school education. Amit was the most popular boy in the school. He had the best sense of humour and a sharp wit. His flawless mimicry and quirky one-liners would leave even the most foul-tempered teachers in splits. Needless to say, *Ami* was the class favourite.

It was after an awfully long time that Abhishek had discovered Amit. The fellow had just vanished after graduating from the school, like many of his ex-classmates did, only to resurface that day all of a sudden, in the most unlikely of places.

"Hey Amit!!" Abhishek called out. But there was no response. The crowd was getting too boisterous and loud.

"*Ami*, hey *AMI*!!!" Abhishek called out again, using the full power of his lungs. And that time it had the desired effect. Amit turned around and had the same look of surprise on his face one has when meeting a former classmate after a gap of many years. Abhishek observed that not much had changed about Amit's appearance; he was still the medium-built guy of average height. The only distinct change was his hair-do; an unruly crop of hair has been replaced by a smart army crew cut. Amit was sharply dressed in a grey pullover teamed with blue denim and sports shoes. He also sported a pair of specs that gave him a sober outlook but the gleam in his eyes betrayed a street-smart attitude.

"Abhishek Baruah? Is it really you!?" Amit exclaimed, oblivious to the crowd around him. "It has been so long, great to see you after an awfully long time. You look pretty much the same like you did back in school. Still the round-faced curious-eyed backbencher, though I must say you are following my hair style. But I think you grew just a shade taller than me, and you must be eating well because you look plump. Now don't just stare at me, come and give me a hug. I can't believe that I am meeting you here of all places."

Abhishek just smiled warmly and gave a hug to his former classmate. Pleasantries exchanged, they discussed about their work and plans in Delhi.

"I didn't know you are in Delhi. Last I heard about you was that you were pursuing graduation from Cotton College in Guwahati. After that nobody knew where you disappeared. So, when did you come to Delhi and where have you been?" Abhishek inquired.

"I took a sabbatical after completing my graduation. I needed a break and also wanted to tour places in India. So, I sort of became a flaneur, a nomadic wanderer, and wandered all over the country for three years to soak the sights and culture of this land."

"You took a break, for three years! Just to be a backpacker and travel around? I can't believe it."

"Well I guess I do have a streak of madness in me. I like the unpredictable and being impulsive. A normal and regular life is for boring people chained by their destiny. Chaos thrills me! A chaotic life with its twists and turns is any day far exciting than a mundane, mechanical existence."

"But still, three years?"

"That's just me!" Amit chuckled. "After that I took admission in the Faculty of Law, Delhi University. It's my third year in Delhi and also my final year in the law faculty. What about you?"

"It's been a decade for me in Delhi. I did my graduation and post-graduation in English Literature, from Delhi University. I was in Kirori Mal College. I am currently working in an Advertising Company called *Creations*; it is located in Okhla Phase 3 near the *subzi mandi*."

"Do you like your job?"

"Have to, it pays my salary."

"That does not sound like a very convincing argument. Anyway, where do you put up in Delhi? Okhla is in south and pretty far away from here. You have travelled an awfully long distance today to get hold of a bottle."

"No, no, not at all. You are mistaken; I don't live in south Delhi" Abhishek clarified. "My address is here itself, in Kingsway Camp. I stay in a Paying Guest accommodation at Outram Lines Colony. There are around half a dozen more PG mates in the house. The owners are an old couple, somewhat conservative in matters of drinks and parties but otherwise quite gentle."

"So, you have also come to celebrate the night?" Amit asked.

"Isn't that obvious?" Abhishek grinned in reply. "Just wait here for a couple of minutes; the crowd seems to have thinned out. I will be right back."

Abhishek reached the counter, ordered a bottle and walked back to where his friend was standing. Seeing the bottle in his hands Amit let out a soft whistle.

"Single malt, and an expensive one at that. Somebody is rich."

"You do tend to spend money on special occasions like today," Abhishek replied tad defensively, "But I see you got a bottle as

11

well, and it's quite expensive too."

"You think so?" Amit asked looking at his bottle, "Yea I guess you are right, on special occasions you do tend to spend money. Anyways I should not keep you waiting for long. Your friends must be arriving any minute and you need to be in your PG to receive them. By the way I stay in Vijay Nagar double storey, now since we have met do come to my place sometime."

"Why don't you join me in the celebration tonight? We have met after ages, and tonight is the perfect excuse to get drunk."

"I would have loved to, but I had already made plans earlier to spend the evening with my friends. So, I won't be able to attend your party, I hope you understand. But I am free this weekend. An office-going guy like you would be too tired to join me on weekdays, so let's get together this Friday evening and get wasted. I will message you my address, since we both put up in the north campus, I am sure you won't have any problem locating me."

Abhishek wanted to say that there was no party at his place. To have a party you need friends, and he had none. It would be him alone, celebrating the last day of the year by himself. But he was embarrassed to admit that he had changed little since his school days. He was still apprehensive of socialising with other people. Besides, Amit already had a party of his own and he didn't want to gate-crash it either.

"Ok, that sounds fine. So, this Friday we revive old memories," Abhishek agreed.

"Sure pal, and a Happy New Year to you in advance! Enjoy the party," Amit cheered. They exchanged their contact numbers, hugged once again in the sheer delight of meeting an old friend after a long time and went their respective ways.

***

A week had gone by since then, and it was Friday again. Abhishek headed straight to Amit's apartment from his office. There were so many things to discuss and so many old memories to revive, he thought. He had called up Amit during lunch hour in office. Amit briefed him on the address and told him to reach as early as possible. As a security measure, Amit even messaged Abhishek the details on his cell phone in case he couldn't note it down properly.

Abhishek may have been in Delhi for nearly a decade, but he never went anywhere outside of Kingsway camp, colloquially known as the north campus. Other than his PG in Outram Lines and the nearby Vishwavidyalaya Metro Station he hardly knew the locality. His first three years in Delhi were spent on his way between the college and the PG. He never went anywhere after his classes. At the most he would go to watch a movie at the nearby movie hall but even that was rare. Abhishek was aware of his shortcomings but all his efforts to rectify his lifetime's habit were in vain. Lacking the will power to fight alone, he resigned to his fate and allowed his life to take its own course. At times he wished he had somebody he could lean on for support; but that wish was never granted. Abhishek fancied his existence similar to that of a creeper whose tendrils needed to latch onto stronger plants to grow and prosper. He was weak and he needed somebody strong to prop him up. He hated the thought but knew it was the truth.

After a harrowing metro ride from the office, Abhishek was standing at Vishwavidyalaya station fighting cold and fatigue. He checked his watch once again, he realized he had been standing there for nearly half an hour. Abhishek decided to take matters into his own hands. He made his way to the nearest wine shop, purchased a bottle and started walking towards Vijay Nagar colony. On his way, he encountered a street urchin sitting on the sidewalk and blowing furiously into an empty polythene packet clutched tightly in his fists. The air around him reeked strongly of adhesive but the little boy was oblivious to his surroundings. The poor boy must have been handed some money by magnanimous revellers on New Year's Eve but the supposed act of kindness was doing him more harm than good. Abhishek just shook his head in amazement and continued walking.

Abhishek crossed the SBI ATM near Hudson Lines and got confused. Amit had messaged him that his apartment is located near a south Indian restaurant named *Udupi*. The problem was he had no idea where *Udupi* was or how to get there. He wanted to call up Amit for directions but was too embarrassed. He decided to ask the locals for help instead, after a lot of misdirection and detours Abhishek finally managed to find his way through the maze of buildings and reached *Udupi*. Not willing to take further undue risks, he finally decided to give Amit a call.

"Hey Amit, Abhishek here. There is a slight hiccup. I have managed to reach *Udupi* but I have no idea where your apartment is and I don't want to get lost again."

There was a light chuckle on the other end as Amit reacted in disbelief. "Are you saying that despite staying in north campus for years you never set foot in Vijay Nagar?"

"Yes, you got it right. I have never been to Vijay Nagar before. Now please be kind enough to come down to *Udupi* as quickly as you can. My hands are aching from carrying the bottle all the way from Kingsway Camp to here."

"Carrying the bottle all the way? Wait a minute, you don't mean to say that you..."

"Yes, I walked down from there. Now please hurry and be quick." Abhishek barely finished his sentence when he heard a loud and distinct laughter from the other end.

"You are such a sorry character! Wait there for five minutes I will be there in a jiffy," Amit hung up.

Tired, exhausted and fed up with the events in the past one-hour, Abhishek lit up a cigarette to de-stress himself. Somebody once told him that when a person lights up a cigarette it is his existence that is burning, not the cigarette. Abhishek merely paid lip service to the advice and continued smoking whenever he felt lonely, upset or simply out of habit. Abhishek had just finished smoking when Amit arrived.

"Are you mad? Why did you not call me if you did not know the way?" Amit asked bluntly.

"I... just did not want to trouble you unnecessarily. I thought you may not want to come out to Kingsway Camp. So, I decided to try it out myself."

"Did it help you? The problem with you is that you think too much. At times you should just speak your mind without taking too much time to think. But first things first, there is a nice Hyderabadi restaurant in the next lane. Let's go there and order something for dinner and get some snacks to go along with the drink. Nice choice of liquor by the way."

"Yea, I thought you would like it. The bottle I mean."

"Of course, I do! It will be easier washing off the dust that had gathered on our old memories." Amit tried to lighten up the mood of his friend but his words did not have the desired effect.

At a small makeshift restaurant, a stone-throw away from *Udupi,* Amit ordered the food, paid the bill and asked the order to be delivered to his apartment.

"Ok, our work is done here. There is enough drinking water and cigarettes at my place to last the night. I think we should get going now." Amit led the way as Abhishek followed him.

There were many lanes intersecting each other with smaller lanes and by lanes seemingly leading to nowhere.

"How the hell do you manage not to get lost in this labyrinth? All the roads and alleys look the same to me. And these buildings, not only the exterior but I am sure the interior designs are the same for every single one of them. Everything must have been designed by the same architect. It all looks the same to me." Abhishek could not control his irritation, which amused Amit.

"I have a knack of finding my way even in a dead-end." Amit remarked lightly.

A couple of minutes later they reached a ragged nondescript building. Abhishek followed Amit through the dimly lit corridor to the flight of stairs. An overpowering stench of cow dung hung in the air which reached Abhishek's nostrils, forcing him to use the faint light of his mobile phone to guide his steps as he carefully treaded on the floor. After walking through the steps for three floors, they reached Amit's apartment.

The apartment is a simple one: a single room set with an attached kitchen and bathroom. Amit's apartment was the first of a total three apartments lined across a narrow corridor which also doubled up as a balcony for the tenants staying there. There was not much to see from the balcony though, just the rooftops of other buildings in the vicinity and the road below. The interior space of the apartment was neither too small nor big; it was just enough for a single individual. The living space in Abhishek's PG was bigger but there were more beds and furniture as well. The space in Amit's apartment was filled up by a wooden bed, a grey-coloured steel *almirah*, a study table and two red colour plastic chairs.

The walls inside were coloured in pale yellow, in contrast to the dark blue painted outside. A tube light and a CFL bulb were responsible for providing light inside the apartment. The paint at some places was chipping off, the kitchen and bathroom walls were painted in white. The floor was simple concrete instead of tiles or marble he had seen in other accommodations. Amit's room was a complete mess, something he took great pride in. The walls were bare of any posters or graffiti but the absence was filled up by dust and cobwebs that decorated the four corners of the ceiling. There was dust everywhere; on the walls, on the floor, over the books etc. The clothes were not ironed and some of it was piled upon one of those plastic chairs and the rest were strewn upon the bed. The books were equally distributed among the study table, the second plastic chair and the bed. To complete the picture the pillow cover was idly hanging by the edge of the study table.

Abhishek was thankful that he was residing in a PG and not left to fend for himself like Amit. Amit hastily emptied both the chairs by dumping their belongings on one side of the bed. He next cleared the other half to make space, then arranged both the chairs and brought them together near his bed. He made Abhishek sit on one chair and on the other one he placed the bottle of whiskey and a bottle of drinking water. The ashtray and packet of cigarettes were placed on the bed along with a lighter. It was not the best seating arrangement available but it hardly mattered. With both of them now settled the two sat down to drink.

"Where am I supposed to sleep?" Abhishek inquired.

"Oh! Don't worry. I have an extra mattress, blanket and pillow which I can place on the floor. Enough space for you to lie down and sleep. There is no bed sheet though, so you will have to adjust and manage," Amit replied.

"You have quite a fine apartment I must say. It's a good thing that you do not have girls staying in the other apartments on this floor. They would have freaked out if they ever caught a glimpse of your living quarters," Abhishek continued after taking a sip.

"Girls do not stay on this floor but we guys have female visitors on a regular basis. They have seen my room up and close. Some of the girls are indifferent and in fact few even like it. But I never bother with public opinion. If you worry about what others think about you then you will never be happy."

"Sounds like a good motto. I guess the old adage is true; homemaking is not really a man's forte. I think only marriage can set you straight. Left to your own devices you will go insane."

"This is precisely the reason why I don't intend to get married. I value my freedom immensely to compromise it over marriage," Amit replied in mock rhetoric.

The Falling Leaf | Aavinash Chaliha

There was a light knock on the door and Amit rose to answer the call. It was the delivery boy who had arrived with the order they had placed at the Hyderabadi restaurant. Amit took the package and bid the boy adieu.

"You should try the *Chicken 65* they make, it is heavenly. Let me just get a plate from the kitchen." Amit got a plate, quickly re arranged the things kept on the chair and resumed the conversation.

"Like I was saying, I never want to marry because I do not want to lose my individuality. I enjoy the company of girls but I hate the shackles of responsibility," Amit continued.

"But you were quiet a romantic in school. Remember how you were caught writing a love letter for that teacher you had a crush on? But thanks to your witty humour, you managed to wriggle your way out of trouble," Abhishek countered.

"First of all, she was the crush of the whole school and not just me. I think she chose the wrong profession. She should have been a model, she was fucking hot. Secondly, I believe she secretly enjoyed the attention and admiration for her from the students. That's why she did not take any punitive measures after catching me red-handed writing that letter. Women, irrespective of their stature, will always feel flattered by compliments. Compliment women, please them with your charm, and shower them with the right kind of attention. They love it!"
"That's your experience talking, I guess."

"No, that's a couple of pegs whiskey down my throat talking." Amit quipped and broke into peals of laughter as Abhishek watched dumbstruck.

The night passed away discussing the old days; the teachers they had a crush on, the various cliques in the school, the notorious students and their infamous incidents, loitering in front of the famous girls' schools that neighboured them, the pros and cons of them studying in a boy's school etc.

***

Friday evenings became an unofficial get-together for the duo. It became a regular affair for the next few weeks with the night being spent drinking at Amit's apartment. The funny thing was that neither of the two were close friends during their school days. They were class mates acquainted with each other but they were as different as chalk and cheese.

"So, tell me about your girlfriends, how many have you had so far?" Amit asked Abhishek during one of their Friday drinking sessions.

"I don't have a girlfriend. I feel awkward approaching girls."

"Why?"

"I don't know. Maybe because I studied in a boys' school and had no contact with girls"

"In case you forgot I also studied in a boys' school. I have no problems approaching girls."

"I just feel apprehensive. I might do something stupid."

"Ok, if not a stable relationship, did you ever have sex with anybody? I mean any flings or one-night stands?"
"No, didn't have sex either." Abhishek replied, somewhat uncomfortable with the question and Amit doubled up with laughter.

"You can't be serious!" Amit exclaimed. "You mean to say you are still a virgin? How old are you?"

"What's so wrong about being a virgin?" Abhishek defended himself. "There are many people in my age group who are virgins, nothing odd about it. What about you, any girlfriends so far?"

"No girlfriends for me! I hate the emotional baggage they carry along with them. I want a no-frills relationship. I tried dating a girl in my graduation days back in Guwahati, but she got serious and wanted commitment. I simply told her to buzz off. One-night stands suit me more, I just have sex when I feel lonely. When I joined law faculty I dated a senior. It was a purely physical relationship for a week, after that we got bored of each other and parted ways. But then there were so many people you could choose from. I have been in many such relationships with different girls over the last couple of years. It is much better than having to see a single girl every day."

"Good for you," Abhishek muttered, "So, do you end up having sex with every girl you meet?"

Amit had a good laugh at the question. "No idiot! What do you take me for? I have many girls in my friend circle, they are just good friends and I share a cordial relationship with them. Then there are some girls who are 'friends with benefits' and other girls you meet in clubs and parties, and you click. It's not like I run after every girl holding my dick."

"Now you are giving me a complex. I wish I could live your life for a day," Abhishek remarked ruefully, envious of Amit's luck with girls.

"It's never too late. Go to pubs and parties etc. try your luck and who knows, you might end up with a girl in your bed."

"But what are the chances that she will definitely sleep with me? What if she just walks off saying she has some urgent work to attend?"

"It's a chance you have to take, depends on how you manage your affairs. Impress her with your personality. Seduce her with your words like I do."

"It is better I invest in a prostitute, at least I will be assured of having sex with her," Abhishek replied in mock-seriousness.

"Not a bad idea, provided you do not feel apprehensive visiting a brothel. I visited a brothel once. The experience could be unnerving for an amateur but it did not discourage me. The environment was disgusting to say the least."

"I don't understand why people agree to pay money for it if it's so much trouble."

"Different people different tastes"

"I can bring a girl to your room if a situation arises, can't I?"

"Sure, why not? Just negotiate a fair price. Unlike you I am not drawing a salary and I have to take these things into consideration." Amit laughed in response.

Abhishek contemplated the offer but did not suggest anything. The night was spent drinking like they always did.

***

CHAPTER-2

The months had gone by, and the winter chill of Delhi was replaced by the gentle footprints of spring. By the month of April, both friends gradually got busy and more involved in their respective careers. Abhishek was bogged down with work and Amit graduated from the Faculty of Law and started his internship under a reputed lawyer practising in the Delhi High Court.

Abhishek always had a dream, of being a writer. Since his childhood he loved reading short stories and novels. Literature offered him a safe sanctuary. For him it was an escape from reality and all the miseries associated with it. Abhishek felt a closer proximity to the make-believe world of imagination etched in ink than the world he inhabited. Books gave him company where human connect was missing. The writings of other authors inspired him to create his own perfect world. In it he was a confident man who always got what he wanted; he was a man society would look up to. That was the comfort he derived in his world of imagination.

His father, of whom Abhishek was greatly terrified, would sternly rebuke him for his hallucinations. But Abhishek was addicted to his imaginary alternate reality where everything was under his control. Abhishek wanted to tell stories of his own but he was afraid of people's reactions. An inner voice, which would sometimes speak to him, would gently persuade Abhishek to take the leap but he would not budge. But after days of intense internal turmoil, Abhishek decided to give in to his impulse. Abhishek did not dare to share his work with a publisher; instead he uploaded them on the internet.

Abhishek had no illusions of grandeur about the quality of prose in front of him but that did not hinder his enthusiasm. He had managed to create something of his own, and for a short instant, reality and his imaginary world was in sync. Abhishek had joined a social networking site which has millions of followers across the globe. In that site there were many online communities for members who had love for literature. Abhishek was a member in one such community and he uploaded his work there. He had read countless stories shared by the group. He liked them, appreciated them and now he hoped that someone else would appreciate his work too.

In the same community page, he saw the post of another member, a girl named Piyushmita Bharali. She worked as a journalist in a leading mainline newspaper in Delhi and had been a regular contributor to the community. Her work was often hailed by the community peers as a masterpiece. Abhishek had read some of her literary pieces before but that time something else caught his eyes.

Piyushmita had updated her profile photo and she looked absolutely stunning. She had the perfect oval face as desired in a girl, auburn shaded lips, and long, curly pitch-black tresses cascading down her shoulders. There was a hint of dimples on her cheeks as she grinned. Her walnut-brown eyes lit up with her smile but they also reflected a steely resolve akin to the eyes of the bird of prey. Abhishek made an effort to read her latest work. It was the story of a strained marriage burdened by extra marital affairs, the ups and downs and the final reconciliation; a marvellous tale, brilliantly narrated. But his mind was fixated on her.

Abhishek could not understand why he never noticed her profile photo before, but he was too distracted right then to worry about that. A voice inside him prodded him further. Goaded by impulse, Abhishek decided to contact her. Before he could hesitate, he mailed his story to her inbox. He wanted a reaction from her; more than that he wanted her to know that a guy named Abhishek existed. Abhishek was surprised by his own audacity, in real life he would break into sweat if he had to get introduced to a girl. But the anonymity of cyberspace had emboldened him. For a moment he acted like a different man, a man more upfront in his actions. After the moment had passed, Abhishek was scared of her reaction but he prayed that things would work his way.

For the next two days Abhishek's mind was a mess. He fumbled and made innumerable mistakes in his work which invited the ceaseless wrath of his boss. Any other day he would have wilted like a dry twig under such scathing criticism but his attention was focused elsewhere. Whenever he got a chance Abhishek would sneak into the social networking site and search for a response. His work was received with lukewarm comments but there was no reply from Piyushmita. Abhishek wanted to push things up a bit. In a move which surprised even him he decided to edit her latest work.

Abhishek liked the flow of language in Piyushmita's narrative, simple yet elegant. But he was disappointed by the conclusion. The idea of a wife forgiving her romantically meandering husband just to save her marriage felt like a clichéd and outdated concept. He decided to write a story on strained relationship himself where a disillusioned wife wanted to break out from a rocky marriage and her philandering husband. Abhishek could not fathom why he was doing all that; he just acted on the orders of his inner voice. He mailed the edited version to her inbox and hoped there would be a response from her side definitely.

The next day, the first thing Abhishek did after reaching office was to check for feedback. He resisted the fear of being caught by his boss and immediately hooked himself on the community page. His prayers were answered. Piyushmita had commented on his work. She had pointed out a couple of grammatical errors and some flaws in the narrative, but over-all she appreciated his effort. Abhishek was elated; it was the best thing that had happened to him in a long time. He wished she could have added a few more lines but he was happy nonetheless because he managed to elicit a response from her. What thrilled him more was the fact that Piyushmita herself had sent him a friend request. Abhishek felt like he had died and gone to heaven.

Over the next few days Abhishek tried interacting with Piyushmita many a time and managed to evoke a response from her occasionally. Abhishek was astonished that he could talk about so many things to a girl he barely knew. Even her deadpan monotonous replies could cheer him up in his most gloomy days. He was falling for her and was thrilled by the idea. He discovered more qualities about her. Abhishek learned that Piyushmita was a versatile writer who could broach on various subjects, a playwright whose plays were enacted at various national venues and an accomplished chess player. Compared to her, he was nothing and his accomplishments were void. Abhishek hoped that their level of interaction would transcend the medium of internet but he had a hunch that she was not so eager on the same.

Abhishek often looked for excuses to talk to Piyushmita. He would seek to consult her for inputs on imaginary stories he would pretend to be working on. This would at times embarrass her and she would reply that she was not that great a writer to counsel others.

"But your writing is as close to perfection as it could be, I am surprised you act so modest." Abhishek entreated her one day.

"I know I am good. I just find it a bother to mentor amateur writers who cannot do simple things on their own. At this level they should know what they are doing."

"I didn't mean to upset you," Abhishek bristled at her comment.

"I am not upset. I find it surprising that you are asking me for inputs. I admired you for taking the initiative to improvise on my work. It showed your confidence. But now you are acting as if you're lost."

"Maybe it was a lucky shot. No, I mean I am working on something more extensive. I don't have experience writing on anything longer than short stories. So, I hoped you could help me with that."

"You work on your draft and mail it to me and I will see if I can do anything."

"Thanks. I do appreciate your help, really."

Abhishek was embarrassed how the conversation eventually shaped up. He had lied about writing extensive stories but he had to say something to get her attention. But then Abhishek was in a fix. He did not have anything to write and if he could not present a draft to her within a reasonable period of time she might construe him as a liar. The probability that she was only being polite in her offer to help never occurred to him. The world of fiction which hitherto was a safe retreat for Abhishek was now closing its walls around him in a pincer movement.

Abhishek decided to search for answers in the realm of ink, and the printed imagination of other authors. He would call in sick for work and spent the entire day reading random stories in the hope that he would be inspired by some idea. It was shallow relief for him. His boss was irate with him for his lackadaisical performance in office and would berate him in front of other employees. Despite all adversities Abhishek persevered and managed to slog out a draft of his new story. It was a pathetic effort by any standards but he sought consolation in the fact that he would not come across as a liar in front of Piyushmita.

On a dull Sunday afternoon, Abhishek mailed a draft of his latest work. By co-incidence, Piyushmita happened to be online that time and she messaged him.

"You have an unusual style of spending your Sunday afternoon."

"Hey! Why do you say that?" Abhishek was surprised by her online presence but he managed to pull in a response.

"You have been working lately. I just got your mail."

"I had a word to keep. Now I feel proud of my effort."

"Why is that? I was expecting to come across your work a little late. Anyway, I will be busy with office work for the next few days. So, you will have to wait."

"As you wish." Abhishek was deflated but he did well to conceal his disappointment.

"So normally how do you spend your Sundays?"

"I read, if not then I go to sleep."

"That doesn't sound too exciting."

"Maybe I am not so exciting a person," Abhishek commented drily.

"This is interesting. I discover something new about you every time we have a conversation."

"What about you, how do you prefer to spend your free time?"

"I try new things. I am recently hooked to painting. I want to learn a musical instrument; I love drums so I guess I will play that. I have managed to gather some of my friends and plan to go on a long excursion sometime next month, and I want to learn Parkour. I heard Parkour gives you a good adrenaline rush."

"Wow, it's quite a list. Now you make me feel insignificant."

"If you think of yourself in some way, then chances are you will end up that way. So, if you think you are insignificant you will end up being insignificant."

The conversation was getting too painful for Abhishek. He got nostalgic of the time when Piyushmita used to give monosyllable replies, at least she was cordial. In a valiant effort to mollify his hurt pride, Abhishek tried one last tactic.

"I know a thing or two about painting, so, if you need help then I will be happy to assist. Besides, I don't find it a bother to help others in their new endeavours." The barb in the last sentence was deliberately placed by Abhishek. It was a subtle, sub-conscious attempt to get back at Piyushmita – the girl who so disdainfully crushed his overtures.

"Is it true?" Piyushmita was taken aback at the revelation.

"I assure you it is true to the best of my knowledge."

Abhishek's claim at being a good painter was a half-truth. While it was true that he was a skilled child prodigy who had a lot of potential, it was also a fact that due to a tragic chain of events he had to divorce himself from his first love. For Abhishek, life had come to a halt back then. The suffocating trauma of painful childhood memories were something that Abhishek always wanted to exorcise, but, so far, he had failed to get rid of them. It was a dark chapter in his life which he found agonising to think about.

"So, tell me Mr. Painter. What do I need to get started?"

Abhishek was woken from his reverie by the sound of beep produced by Piyushmita's message.

"A brush, colours, pencil, paper, acrylic, canvas and stuff like that."

"That was helpful. Okay mister, I got other work to do. See you later, Tchao!"

The conversation was a hurting experience for Abhishek. He was aware of the anomalies in their respective personalities but today the dialogue felt excruciating. The more he talked to her the more his insignificance came to the fore. He expected a kind word from her, some appreciation even, but all he earned was her ridicule. He never felt himself so inconsequential. Inspired by a hurt ego, of which he had not being conscious of for many years, Abhishek decided to make a few changes in his life. He vowed to start life anew from where he had stopped. What happened so many years back was a big blow to his tender psyche and he had been a prisoner of those painful memories ever since. But now Abhishek was determined to break free.

***

It has been years since Abhishek held a brush in his hands, he had never felt inclined to creative arts again after he quit. He had an uncanny talent for creativity which he had buried with his own hands. But after the recent conversation with Piyushmita an old spark re-ignited in him. Abhishek felt motivated to pursue his love for creativity with renewed vigour. It would be a tedious and time-consuming effort but he was determined to recover lost ground. Abhishek got hold of all the essential items needed for his newly re-discovered passion and devoted his free time perfecting it.

With the first swirl of brush against the canvas, a yearning long since subdued exploded with a vengeance in his sentience. A vague familiar feeling of happiness which he once experienced years ago was slowly taking over him. Life had been monochrome for too long, Abhishek decided to add some colour into it.

***

CHAPTER-3

It had been a while since Abhishek visited Amit. Amit was now a partner at a reputed law firm and he was busy working on a new case. The duo had been in contact through text messages but nothing more than that. Abhishek decided to visit Amit on the coming weekend to make up for lost time. Further he sent a text message telling his friend that there was an urgent business and they must meet.

Abhishek had a nagging feeling that he won't be able to keep in touch with Amit for long. He had valid reasons for believing so. There have been speculations in his office that *Creations* was planning to explore the North-East Indian market for which they would be opening an office in Guwahati. If the rumours were true Abhishek was pretty sure then he might get a transfer offer to Guwahati or at the very least he would be asked by his boss if he would be interested to move in there. It made sense, because, doing so would save the company time and effort in hiring a new resource. Abhishek had mixed feelings about moving back to Guwahati, on one hand he wanted to make a visit to the place where he had grown up but at the same time the thought also filled him with trepidation. Guwahati held some painful memories for him. Abhishek involuntarily laughed at the complicated paradox of his life.

Abhishek knew that if he was offered a transfer then he would take it. He had been contemplating shifting back to Guwahati, not because of his free will but due to other compulsions. Being the only child in the family he had certain familial obligations which he could not choose to ignore even if he wanted to. For the past one year his father would often call him up and complain of poor-health. He had been considering moving back to Guwahati for some time, but could not do much because of the bleak job scenario back home. It was not possible for him, being in Delhi, to look for a suitable job elsewhere. At the same time, he could not take the risk of resigning from his job and moving back to Guwahati without any back up plan. He searched for advertising firms in Delhi who have branches in Guwahati but without luck. The talk of *Creations* opening a branch would be once in a lifetime opportunity. It was an opportunity he could not afford to miss.

Abhishek did not know how many more days he would be staying back in Delhi if the offer came up. But they would give him three weeks at least or so, he hoped. He once discussed with Amit about their respective futures in Delhi. Amit had made it clear that he had come to Delhi to stay. He would be working here and settle down in this city in future. Abhishek had confessed that he might have to leave Delhi behind one day but he was not sure when. He had no idea that he could be going back so soon. He decided to wait and verify the veracity of the rumours first. Only after the rumours were confirmed, he could prepare for his long journey back home.

One Friday afternoon, his boss Joseph Anand, a no-nonsense man in his late forties, called Abhishek to his cabin. With a heavy-built and over six feet in height, Joseph had an imposing physical presence in the office. The employees were at an awe of him and his mere words were construed as verbal commands. Despite his daunting stature, Joseph was a fair judge of character and lavish with his praise for those who stood up to his expectations.

"I think you must be aware of the rumours of *Creations* opening a branch in Guwahati?" Joseph began without any preamble.

"Yes sir, I have heard about such rumours."

"Then you must have also presumed, or at least given a thought, that you may be asked if you want to take a transfer?"

"Yes sir. The thought did cross my mind."

"You are correct in both your assumptions. We are opening a

branch in Guwahati and the management has put forward your name as the best possible candidate to be posted there. Your hometown is Guwahati and you have been working with us for quite a long time, you would be the perfect choice. But I want to know your decision first, make up your mind and let me know post-lunch."

"Yes sir. I will apprise you about my decision." Abhishek paused for a moment to check if his boss had anything more to say. As he was about to leave Joseph called out again.

"Abhishek, there is one more thing I forgot to mention. I had a conference-call with the Managing Director of *Chopra & Chopra Enterprises*. They have assigned us a new project and want the results within two weeks. I wanted you to get started on it immediately, I am personally supervising the work and I want daily evaluations. Now go and get on to it."

"Yes, sir I will." Abhishek managed to walk out before his boss could fire any more orders at him.

In the advertising world, when there was no workload, the office hours were easy, but when there was work, it transformed into one of the busiest places on earth. Abhishek knew that his plan of making it to Amit's place in the evening had gone for a toss. Deadlines were sacrosanct and took precedence over everything else. He and his team would have to stay back and work late night shifts. In the course of next two weeks he and his team would scarcely have time to eat in office. There would be brainstorming sessions, paperwork, draft, re-draft and sending it to the client for approval on almost a daily basis. If needed, be he would have to come to office on weekends and complete the project before deadline. For the next fortnight, there would not be any social life for any of his team members. It would be work and more work, nothing else. Abhishek sent a text message to Amit explaining that due to unavoidable work pressure, the plans for the evening had been cancelled.
Abhishek had more things to worry about other than the current project. It was his proposed transfer which made him anxious.

Ideally, he would have loved to meditate on the subject for at least two days before coming to a decision. But his boss forced him to give an answer post lunch that day. At times, he hated himself for being so soft-spoke. Amit was right; at times a person should simply speak out his mind without fear. It was then he realized that he might be leaving Delhi without meeting Piyushmita even once. He was still smarting from her comments but he could not detach himself from the girl. Like a vine which needed external support to mature and sustain itself, Abhishek needed Piyushmita to survive.

In desperation he pulled out his mobile phone and frantically searched for her number. A few seconds had passed before he remembered that she had never shared her number with him. She had not been online as well for the past few days either. It seemed that everybody had become busy with their work at the same time. There was nothing much Abhishek could do besides cursing his fate.

Post lunch, Abhishek went to his boss' cabin and apprised him of his decision. Abhishek let his boss know that he was willing to take up the offer of moving to Guwahati. Joseph simply nodded his head in approval and asked him to continue working on the latest project. Having agreed to be transferred to Guwahati meant that Abhishek must now also prepare the handover for the next person to be placed in charge in lieu of him. Abhishek felt exhausted already, life was never easy.

For the next two weeks Abhishek's waking hours were spent on working and re-working on the project, preparing the handover for his replacement and fighting fatigue. Joseph informed Abhishek that he would be leaving for Guwahati by the last week of July, two weeks after the deadline of *Chopra & Chopra Enterprises* assignment. After a rigorous two weeks of sleep- deprived labour, Abhishek and his team finally completed the project assigned to them by Friday noon. Abhishek also successfully logged down and handed over his client profile and Key Responsibility Area to his next in line. It was a well-earned break for him and he decided to celebrate it at Amit's place in the evening. Abhishek pulled out his mobile and dialled Amit's number. After a couple of rings Amit responded.

"Hello Abhishek! Been a long time, how are you?"

"I am doing good, hope you are fine as well. I have been thinking that it's been a while since we both sat down for a drink. Today is Friday, are you free in the evening?"

"I wish I could have said yes, but unfortunately I have made some prior commitments. I am sorry I won't be free today. But you are right it's been a long time since we both got drunk. Do one thing, you come to my place tomorrow afternoon."

"You want to get drunk in the afternoon?" Abhishek was astonished.

"What's the problem? Tomorrow is Saturday and day after is Sunday. You don't have to go to office either day so you don't need to worry about a hangover. Ultimately you should you get a high, what does it matter whether it is evening or afternoon? Come to my place on Saturday, we will have lunch and then booze."

"Fine then, Sunday afternoon is decided," Abhishek replied.

Abhishek sat back on his chair and relaxed. Sitting relaxed doing nothing in office after two weeks of back-breaking labour seemed surreal. He lay back against the backrest and closed his eyes for a few blissful minutes. But the thought of not meeting Piyushmita continued to bother him. There was no way he could possibly contact her over the phone and neither had she been coming online of late. Abhishek suddenly felt a creeping uneasiness in him. He was starting to feel restless. He looked at his watch once, it was four in the afternoon. Abhishek decided to leave early that day; a few swirls from his brush might soothe his frayed nerves. Abhishek knocked at the door of his boss' cabin and called in sick, requesting for the day off. Joseph who was busy fiddling on his computer arched his eyebrows and looked up. His sceptical gaze attested the fact that he saw through the ruse. But Joseph was in a lenient mood and sanctioned his leave.

Abhishek walked out of his office, lit a cigarette and started walking towards Govindpuri metro station. A thousand thoughts played in his mind. The thought of going back to Guwahati - a city he tried to run away from, his ambitions about Piyushmita, the renaissance of his long-forgotten passions and thoughts about his future all joined hands to suffocate him with perturbation. Unable to come to a solution, he continued walking and did not even realize when he reached the metro station. Abhishek went through the daily routine of security checks and navigating through the crowds to the platform. It was the same rush and madness once the train arrived. The passengers seemed to derive some primeval thrill in contesting for seats. It was a credit to the metro authorities that no riots had broken out inside the station. Abhishek was slowly getting habituated to the rush but never enough. After a long, congested ride he finally reached Vishwavidyalaya station.

As he was walking towards his PG in Outram Lines, Abhishek felt his mobile phone ring. He pulled out the phone and was surprised to find Amit's number flashing on the screen.

"Hey Abhishek, sorry to call you during office hours. But there is a slight change in the plans. I am home early today. There is no need to wait till tomorrow. If you are willing we can sit for drinks today evening."

Abhishek was surprised at this sudden turn of events and could not control his curiosity. "This is great, but what happened to your previous plans?"

"It's a long story. I will be sharing the details with you once you reach my place. What time are you going to leave office today?"

"As a matter of fact, I already left the office and I am standing near Vishwavidyalaya station. I was on my way to Outram Lines when you called."

"That's incredible. Now do one thing, forget Outram Lines and head straightaway to Vijay Nagar. Don't bother stopping by at the wine shop. I already had got the bottle in my room and have ordered for the snacks and dinner."

"Since when did you start stockpiling alcohol?"

"I do not stockpile alcohol you idiot. I will tell you everything once you show up. Hurry now."

Amazed at the sudden development Abhishek decided to visit Amit and find out the reason for that sudden change of plans. Besides, he thought, it was also the opportune moment to share about the latest development in his career, with Amit. Abhishek called for a rickshaw and soon enough he was in Vijay Nagar. He paid the fare and straightaway headed to Amit's room. Abhishek gave a light knock on the door.

"Come in! The door is open"

"Hey Amit, it's good to see you after a long time."

"Same here. Pull that chair near the study table and have a seat."

Abhishek pulled the chair and was surprised to see the books on the study table kept in a more organised manner. Abhishek looked around the room, something was amiss.

"You cleaned your room?" He asked Amit.

"Is it that obvious?" Amit started laughing.

"Of course, it is! It looks clean and fresh. Did I miss out on your birthday or something?"

"No, not birthday. I was expecting a guest. And to put your imagination to rest let me confess. It is a girl."

"Now I understand what you were so busy at! But what made you change your plans all of a sudden?"

"First things first. Let us arrange the bottle, glasses and the chairs. We both share a drink first and then we talk. Food has already been ordered and it should arrive any minute."

Abhishek pulled in the other chair as Amit got the bottle of water, whiskey and two glasses. Amit had poured the first peg when the delivery boy arrived, the parcel was taken and the boy was paid and he went off his way.

"Now, where was I? Yeah. She was supposed to come but for some unavoidable reasons she could not make it." Amit replied with a mischievous grin. Before Abhishek could ask further, Amit fished out his cell phone from his pocket and showed him a text message which read, *'Catastrophe! I can't make it today'*.

Abhishek was still puzzled, even worried. "What did she mean by *catastrophe*? I hope she has not met with an accident or something like that."

"Oh, she is perfectly fine. Just that she was supposed to spend the night with me. But it's that time of the month, you know, and we had to call off the arrangement," Amit replied matter-of-factly.

Abhishek was dumbfounded, unable to fathom the meaning behind the words. Then it struck him and he was flustered. "You rascal, that's why you were unwilling to meet me earlier. For how long do you know this girl?"

"It's been almost a year. We have been together many times and tonight would have been the same but for the unavoidable circumstance. In fact, we both had celebrated the New Year's Eve together in this very room."

"New Year's Eve? That would be the day I met you outside the wine shop. But you said you would be having a party at your place. There must have been a lot of people around."

"I did have a party, just not the way you assumed."

"You really have a way with girls, don't you?"

"You can just say that I have been lucky in such matters!" Amit laughed.

"Yea I know you are lucky with girls, you told me so. Right now, I am going through a tricky phase. I am leaving Delhi after two weeks. There is a new branch opening in Guwahati and I have been assigned there." Abhishek revealed as he took a sip.

"Now you leave me stunned! Are you posted there on a temporary basis, say like six months or are you going to be permanently based there?"

"I think it is a permanent arrangement. The offer is not bad, the pay is good and I will be the one in charge. I don't have to bother too much about expenses back there as compared to Delhi. I have been in this city long enough, its time I moved back home."

"How many people would be there?"

"Me, an intern and other support staff."

"Isn't that too small a number to function properly?"

"Not really. We will be in constant touch with the main office in Delhi; any bulk work would be sorted out in co-ordination with them. It's not scary as you think, not in this day and age of internet connectivity."

"Hmm! Fine then, will you take a flight or are you going by train?"

"By train. There is simply too much luggage to be carried in the flight. I will be travelling by Rajdhani, First Class."

"You got your tickets done?"

"I will. I had called up the travel agent for the same."

"Travel agent? Your company is not booking your tickets?"

"No. But they will reimburse the full amount in my coming month's salary."

"Ok but why do you sound upset? You sound like you have fallen in love with somebody here and you don't want to leave her and go."

Alcohol mixed with anxiety almost made Abhishek confess his dilemma about Piyushmita to Amit. But he just managed to restrain himself.

"No, not at all. You are just misinterpreting what I said. Maybe it's just that I have stayed for so long here in the same place. I will miss the guys in my PG and office, and of course you."

"Is that all? This is what's making you so sad? Dude, don't be so childish! You are going to Guwahati, not some battlefield. It is not like we will never hear from you again or vice versa. Go home enjoy yourself and when you feel like, you can come to Delhi. It is not like you require a passport and visa to come here and nobody in Delhi you know is going anywhere, at least not me."

"I guess you are right. I can always come to Delhi when I want." Abhishek agreed, feeling somehow buoyed by Amit's words.

"I know I am right. You will be leaving Delhi in two weeks, which is next to next Friday. So, in the coming two weekends we will arrange a grand farewell for you. We will make you some memories. There is this Bollywood action movie which hit the screens today. It's too late to go now, but we can watch it tomorrow morning first show in Ashok cinema hall. And since you confessed that you are unfamiliar with Delhi I take it on myself to be your tour guide."

"Tours are fine. But the movie you are talking about, I have read the reviews. The movie is shit! I am not going to watch that movie."

"It is not about the movie you dimwit. It's about going out and having a good time. When was the last time you watched a movie in a single screen hall instead of a multiplex?"

"It's been some time," Abhishek conceded. "The last time I watched a movie in Ashok was during my University days. Once I started earning it has always been the multiplex for me."

"Watching a movie in a single screen hall has its own thrill," Amit explained. "The reaction of the public; the whistles, cat calls, applause, abuses for bad performance etc. all make for a grand carnival atmosphere. The experience of watching the movie, instead of the movie, becomes more exciting. You don't get this sort of ambience in a multiplex."

"Yes, I mean who can argue with facts like that?" Abhishek remarked sarcastically which only made Amit laugh.

"Stop thinking so much all the time. At times you should be part of the crowd. Anyway, let's enjoy the drink for now. We will talk about movies and places tomorrow." Amit changed the topic.

The night was spent drinking.

*

CHAPTER-4

The next morning, Abhishek woke up at around ten. He along with Amit went downstairs to a nearby *dhaba* to have breakfast. The *dhaba* was nothing more than a sturdy table placed underneath a tarpaulin. On the table was a two-burner gas stove, on one burner tea was prepared and on the other *parathas* were being baked relentlessly. Two wooden benches facing each other were placed perpendicular to the table. The *dhaba* was special because it was open 24 hours and was immensely popular with the students from the University. The family running the business kept serving tea and *parathas* regardless of the hour.

Amit ordered for two cups of tea and two *parathas*. Amit was at ease with his surroundings, chatting with the man baking *parathas*, as Abhishek looked on. Soon enough more customers started filling in, mostly University students who regularly went there for tea. Abhishek had rarely been to his college canteen when he himself used to be a student. Seeing so many students around him discussing about the latest trends in the campus brought forward old memories in him. Amit in the meantime was sipping tea and having small talk with one of the students with whom he must be acquainted.

Breakfast was over, Amit paid the bill and they both walked towards the rickshaw stand.

"Kingsway Camp?" Amit curtly asked the rickshaw-puller who nodded his head. They both hopped on to the rickshaw and were on the way.

"Why do you look so amazed?" Amit asked, vaguely curious.

"What me?!"

"Yes you."

"I don't know, I mean I can't explain it to you in words. You won't get it."

"Try me."

"Just a trivial matter, when I was in the University I never got a chance to hang out with my classmates like those young fellows back in the *dhaba*. I wonder what it must have felt like to come here late at night with your group of friends for midnight tea. I missed out on a lot of things."

Amit chuckled and gently patted on Abhishek's back. "We all miss out on something or the other and it's a good thing. It makes us who we are. You should not talk like an old man; you have your whole life ahead of you and plenty of opportunities to make new memories. Don't be so stuck in the past."

"I guess you are right."

"I know. I am always right!"

After a ten-minute ride, the rickshaw dropped them at the auto rickshaw stand at Kingsway Camp. Half a dozen autos were lined up, their drivers fanatically calling out to passengers to board their vehicle. Amit and Abhishek boarded one of the *sawari* autos, or one of the shared autos which ferries anywhere between five to eight passengers over short distances.

"How much do these guys charge?" Abhishek asked. Amit gave him an incredulous look.

"You have never been in these autos before?"

"There was never a need to. I walk to the metro; at the most I take the cycle-rickshaw. These things are new to me."

"Dude! I think you need to re-discover Delhi after all these years. So, tell me, where do we start?"

Abhishek was about to protest but Amit cut him short. "Don't fret over small things like expense, leave that to me. After the movie we are going to tour Delhi."

The auto rickshaw started and in a five-minute ride they crossed Outram Lines and Indra Vihar before stopping at *Ashok* cinema hall near Mukherjee Nagar. *Ashok* cinema hall was a relic from the past. In the age of internet where tickets can be booked online they still believed in selling of tickets over the counter. The screen and other facilities inside were just as antiquated, but that did not deter a sizeable crowd from thronging the hall on weekends.

Abhishek checked the time; it showed fifteen minutes to eleven, still another forty-five minutes to go before the movie would start. Amit purchased two tickets and handed one to him. The good thing was that they did not have to worry about a packed crowd near the counter. It seemed like nobody was too interested in watching the movie, but Abhishek knew that footfalls would dramatically rise after eleven. The two of them smoked and chatted as the minutes passed by, patiently waiting for the gates to open so that they could take their seats inside the theatre.

Finally, it was 11:30 am and the gates were open. As Abhishek expected, a fair number of people had gathered. Tickets were sold out in fifteen minutes flat. A shady character was trying his best to sell movie tickets in black to the disappointed fans, while skillfully evading the police constables at the same time. As the minutes ticked by, the crowd further swelled in number. The people were milling near the gate, somehow restrained by the steel gates from crashing in. Abhishek slowly stepped backwards from the growing surge; he thought it would be better to let them enter first than get carried away. His belief was vindicated when the pack of people rushed in frenzy once the gates opened. Abhishek, followed by Amit, entered when the initial madness had subsided.

They took their seats inside the hall. Amit quickly bought a couple

43

of popcorn packets and bottles of cola to last them till the interval. The hall was jam-packed, the crowd impatiently shouted for the movie to start and already abuses were being hurled. Abhishek gently shook his head at the ruckus, but Amit was thoroughly enjoying himself and even shouted words of encouragement to the agitators. At last the lights were turned off and the projector started rolling. The abuses and cuss words were stopped with immediate effect and replaced with loud cheers and whistles. It was almost a riot as the name casting played on the screen on the backdrop of a catchy 'item number' which was immensely popular with the masses. Amit lustily joined in with the rest, furiously clapping and singing along with the public, to hell with melody.

Some of the more enthusiastic members of the audience, drunk on alcohol and hysteria, stood on their chairs and danced along with the song. One fellow in particular got too much into the groove; one hand on his head and the other on his waist he was vigorously swinging his hips in a valiant but hopeless attempt to match the steps of the actress. In spite of himself Abhishek could not help laughing at the antics. He had always viewed the crowd as an instrument of anarchy but that was the first time he witnessed the lighter side and he liked it.

The three hours of the movie continued in the same vein. The hero's introductory scene was received with thunderous applause. Whistles and catcalls abounded when the on-screen couple indulged in passionate lip-locking, jeers and abuses would erupt at the on-screen villain's villainous machinations and more applause would follow at the bombastic dialogues delivered by the lead star. All in all, it was a riveting experience for the audience, especially for Abhishek. He remained subdued throughout the movie, but, in the climax, he was enthralled by the high-octane action scenes and clapped and shouted just as loud as the others.

"So, did you like it?" Amit asked once they walked out of the theatre.

"It was fantabulous! I was wasting my money on multiplexes all these years. I should have never left the single screen. I don't feel like shouting and clapping inside a movie hall when watching any movie, but today was fun. To be honest I don't know why I was even watching such a ridiculous movie, but the public reaction made up for everything."

"I knew you would love the experience. Now for your tour of Delhi, tell me which places would you like to visit?"

"I would love to visit Chandni Chowk. I have heard fabulous stories about the place; its old-world charm, connection to the past, its architecture, its legends, and all the past and forgotten anecdotes associated with it. It is almost like a living entity, I want to experience it."

Amit stared a long look of disbelief at Abhishek. "I knew I should have expected something like this from you. There go all my hopes of partying tonight."

"I have a fascination for history," Abhishek tried to justify his choice.

"You and your morbid obsession with the past! Come now, let's go."

***

The duo made their way to the Vishwavidyalaya metro station where they boarded a train to Chandni Chowk. The ride lasted for approximately ten minutes. Like any regular day there was a sizeable crowd and the accompanying hustle. But Abhishek was getting more at ease with his surroundings and he didn't mind it at all.

A whole new world of sight, sound and smell welcomed him when he emerged out of the Chandni Chowk station. There were narrow congested lanes everywhere which were filled up with people, rickshaws, two-wheelers, four-wheelers, carts, shops, stalls and even more people. There were scores of stalls lined up one after another seemingly losing out in infinity. Almost anything an individual would desire could be brought in the markets of

Chandni Chowk - everyday kitchen appliances, clothing, stationery, electronic goods, jewellery etc.

It was the sight of Chandni Chowk that captured his attention. The first impression of the walled city was staggering. It was a throbbing sea of people. Cyclists and motorists honking and cursing people to get out of the way, pedestrians walking on the streets, beggars squatting on the sidewalks with their arms outstretched shouting for alms, hawkers walking up to pedestrians and imposing irresistible bargains, stall owners selling their wares, customers lining up to buy sweets, street food, locally made handicrafts etc. They were everywhere. Any other day the sight of a teeming crowd would have been enough to nauseate Abhishek but that day his perceptions had changed. He did not feel alienated, for that day he was a part of the crowd. It was an incredulous experience for him, yet fascinating all the same.

A little distance away from the station's exit, a flock of pigeons were huddled together on a pavement and busy pecking on the grains. For no apparent reason they broke away and took flight, some of them though returned while the others went their way. The sight of the pigeons mesmerized Abhishek. Like the people, they were omnipresent in that place and one could find them everywhere. Amit guided Abhishek through one of the many congested lanes. Many people have called Chandni Chowk as the heart of Delhi, Abhishek now understood why. The place was bustling with activity. People were buying and selling things, some even wandered around aimlessly.

"Where do you want to go from here?" Amit enquired.

"Let's go to *Parathe Wale Gali* first. I heard it is the most famous street here."
"As you wish."

They walked through the cramped lanes lined up with eateries as an avalanche of sumptuous aroma greeted their advance.

"The city of old Delhi was known by the name of Shahjahanabad

46

during the Mughal era and the Chandni Chowk market was its most famous legacy. Chandni Chowk was designed and built by Jahan Ara, daughter of the Mughal emperor Shah Jahan. There used to be canals which segregated the markets in those days. It has been said that on moonlit nights the moonlight reflected from the canals would bathe the city in silver light, that's how it got its name Chandni Chowk. Though some people differ in their opinion, according to them the place got its name because it used to be famous for its silver merchandise. This, some people claim, gave the title of *Katra Asharfi* to Chandni Chowk in its early days. Whatever be the case, it is one of the oldest and busiest markets in India. Some of the shops established here are more than hundred years old and still run by the same family. A vivid old-world charm thrives in this place, like time has stood still all these years."

Amit was busy narrating the history of Chandni Chowk to Abhishek who soaked in every word. Abhishek glanced around the place as they walked. The city might have changed over the centuries yet in a miraculous way it was still going in the same vein.

Amit could not resist the temptation of the appetizing fare that overpowered his senses. The two stopped by an old eatery whose owners claimed it was established a century ago. There was not much room inside but it was somehow able to accommodate eight tables. Two cooks worked tirelessly near the lit burners, one pounding the dough and shaping the *parathas* and the other baking it over the pan. An archaic ceiling fan, which probably last saw production during the British Raj, hung low and whirled at a snail's pace in vain attempt to provide relief from the heat. There were no exhaust fans but a couple of Mughal style *roshandans* were expected to let the smoke away.

"Fabulous!" Abhishek commented after taking a view. "The owners should declare their restaurant a heritage site and convert it into a working museum. They will probably mint more money this way."

"Two *parathas* please," Amit ordered the waiter.

They waited for some time until the waiter served them a plate of paratha each with some vegetable curry.

"This tastes wonderful," Abhishek conceded after taking a bite.

"It is called the *Parathe Wale Gali* after all. It has a reputation to preserve. If you want to try out street food then there are a couple of places I know. It may not have the same historical aura of Chandni Chowk but the food is great. Want to go there?"

"Sounds like a good plan. But first we explore a bit. Have you been to Chandni Chowk before?"

"I visited the Red Fort once, does it count?" Amit quizzed sarcastically.

"Let us start again. I bet you will enjoy it."

Amit was not particularly interested in prolonging his stay at Chandni Chowk but he decided to play along.

They crisscrossed through the narrow lanes and by-lanes of the locality. Amit played his part as the tour guide, pointing out to a random *Haveli* and narrating its long-chequered history, of some of the buildings or spots that have stood witness to wars, plunder and other sporadic events in Delhi's history. Most of the original structures had perished due to natural or man-made causes and rest underwent renovations over the centuries but some still remained the same as they once were. It saddened Abhishek to see the famous buildings reduced to tatters or at best pale images of its once glorious self. There were shops and *Havelis* set up when the Mughals were still a respectable power in the sub-continent. These landmarks deserved a better deal he thought.

They next visited the famed Jama Masjid, located at the heart of the old city. The monument was an architectural marvel, but what Abhishek liked best about the place was the tranquility that washed over him. Standing near the entrance to the Masjid he looked out at the walled city.

The extent of Chandni Chowk was visible from the vantage point. The Temples, Gurudwaras, *Havelis*, Bazaars, shops, houses, vehicles and people offered a diverse array of sights that juxtaposed the old with the new. Abhishek tried to imagine how the city would have looked four hundred years back. In his mind's eye he could visualize people in ethnic Indian attire milling around the shops selling and buying wares. The hustle and noise in the market back then must have been the same as it was that day. The *Havelis* that were in tatters now would have exuded pomp and splendor during its heydays. The gates which once guarded the seat of Mughal authority have long eroded in time, exposing the city to outside influences it was unaware of. He tried to locate the co-ordinates of the canals that used to adorn the bazaar. What a sight it must have been to watch the bazaar glow in the rays of the moonlight reflected from the canals!

In between, he could imagine Mughal *sowars* on horseback patrolling the streets of the bazaar. With the trot of their horses, sabres in scabbards dangling by their waist and lances held high the *sowars* must have presented an intimidating yet fascinating sight. Abhishek wondered if the stereotyped description of medieval era Indian bazaars filled with elephants, snake charmers and lean, wiry *fakirs* meditating on a bed of nails had any truth in them. Maybe it was true back then, at least the colonial era British thought so. Abhishek strained his neck to see if some forgotten snake charmer was still trying to charm the cobra with his flute or if an ancient fakir was displaying the great Indian rope trick to a bunch of awestruck tourists.

Chandni Chowk was not segregated from Delhi and it was a part of the twenty-first century milieu, yet there were uncanny dissimilarities between the two that Abhishek could not accurately place. From that vantage point, the city of Delhi metaphorically appeared as an ancient tree to Abhishek. Like an aged tree it had seen many seasons over the millennia from the dawn of the first empire remembered in mythology to the modern age of technology. It had been scarred and sacked in many wars throughout its history but somehow managed to recuperate itself from every disaster; like a tree whose leaves might have shed, branches broken or even the trunk that had been chopped down several times but as long as its roots remained untouched and firmly etched on earth it regenerated over time. The city might be new and changed over the ages, but like those trees, some part of its primeval self still remained buried and unscathed, waiting to be excavated.

Abhishek identified Chandni Chowk as the conduit that connected the modern to the ancient. To him Chandni Chowk in its vibe at least remained constant while the rest of the city moved ahead. Walking on the deserted lanes in a moonlit night he could travel back through the passages of time and get lost in another era. The umbilical cord of the walled city connecting it to its past had not yet fully severed.

The notion of an older version of a city, which was still alive yet forgotten, among the hustle bustle of lanes, buildings and traffic of a more modern city fascinated and amused him. He suddenly felt elated for no obvious reason and smiled. Thoughts were running hard and fast in his mind, but he could not fathom the cause of his joy. Maybe, he thought, in re-discovering this old city he had partially managed to rediscover himself.

Abhishek did not want to leave, he continued to stare spellbound over the horizon. There was something about the place, a mystifying romance which haunted him. He wanted to stay there a bit longer, but he knew that he had to go.

As they were making their exit from Chandni Chowk, Amit stopped by one of the stalls selling locally made handicrafts. Amit returned a while later carrying a small box which was gift wrapped.

"Here, a present for you from me."

"What is inside that?"

"Now that you have asked, it is a miniature clay elephant. Since you are so captivated by memories I felt like it is the most apt souvenir for you."

"Thanks. So where are we heading for right now?"

"To Chittaranjan Park and later to MKT."

***

The two took a cab to CR Park as Amit did not feel like getting pushed and shoved around in a crowded metro coach. Ironically it was Abhishek who then missed the chaos. Halfway through their ride, Amit regretted taking the cab. The traffic jams were long and occurred at every signal, getting stuck in a jam in late afternoon with the sun blazing overhead could be a very agonizing thing during Delhi summer. The effect of the heat and frustration was already showing; tempers were running high and drivers would honk incessantly from their cars inviting sharp abuses from people nearby. Two motorcyclists, feeling that abuses would simply not do, decided to have a go at each other in a no-holds-barred street fight. The rest of the crowd watched indifferently, as though a roadside show was going on, the few who were interested was cheering up the two antagonists.

The joy of the people watching the spectacle was short-lived though. A burly police constable wielding his *lathi* charged at the two street fighters, apparently to stop the fight or give them a good whacking and kill his own boredom. The signal soon turned green and the motorists, along with the audience, had to go their way.

"What a bunch of hooligans?" Abhishek muttered, shocked and disgusted by the sight.

"Ordinary people like you and me, not hooligans. They were just pushed to their extreme by their surrounding and hence their emotions got the better of them. They cannot control the environment, so the environment controls them. It could have been anybody in their place, even us." Amit interjected, giving his opinion on the matter.

"That's a weird philosophy."

"Such is life."

After a long session of halt and drive they finally reached Chittaranjan Park. Chittaranjan Park, colloquially known as CR Park, was home to Delhi's largest concentration of Bengali community and the hub of Bengali culture in Delhi. It did not have an expansive history as Chandni Chowk but it had its own inspiring story of testing times overcome by human grit and struggle.

"What is the specialty of CR Park?" Abhishek inquired.

"The street food, if you have a craving for the spiciest *Jhaal Moorie* and *Puchka* then this is the place for you. Also, the fish cutlets and fish rolls are some of the best you can savor."

After a round of street buffet, the two made their way to MKT.

Amit booked a cab to Majnu Ka Tila, more popularly known by its abbreviation MKT. Majnu Ka Tila, literally meaning mound of Majnu, is a Tibetan residential colony in north Delhi. It was formed after the Dalai Lama escaped into exile in India from Tibet with his followers in 1960. The Tibetan Diaspora was later resettled in this area. MKT was located adjacent to the outer Ring Road, near ISBT Kashmere Gate with the Yamuna River for its neighbor. The colony was officially named as New Aruna Nagar Colony but the name Majnu ka Tila gained more popularity for obvious reasons.
After an hour's journey punctuated by traffic jams they reached their destination.

"Tell me, does the name Majnu in Majnu Ka Tila refer to the infamous lover from Arabian folklore?" Abhishek was both intrigued and amused by the name of the colony and couldn't resist asking the cab driver.

The man laughed at the question. "No sir, the place is actually named after an Iranian Sufi mystic named Abdulla who was deeply devoted to the Sikh Guru, Guru Nanak. When Guru Nanak visited this place, Abdulla would ferry people across the Yamuna River for free as a sign of respect for the Guru. Probably for his unflinching devotion he was named Majnu or mad, and the name stuck. Many people, even most of the Delhiites, think of the love-struck Majnu when they hear the name Majnu ka Tila."

"They are not far off the mark. One turned mad in spirituality, the other turned mad in love." Amit quipped and they both laughed.

"So, what do we have here in the abode of Majnu?" Abhishek turned to Amit.

"It is mostly famous for its Buddhist monastery, shops and stalls selling Tibetan handicrafts and clothes stores where you can strike a good bargain. It is a hot-spot for foreign tourists and students of Delhi University from North Campus. But the reason I keep coming to MKT every now and then is because of its most delicious serving of Tibetan food. Authentic Tibetan cuisines at throwaway prices, what more can a connoisseur ask for?"

"Nothing can keep you away from your love for food!"

"Why would anybody want to be away from food? Come, I know an amazing place where we can sit there and relax. "

The duo walked through the narrow gullies of MKT towards their destination. There was a hint of an incline as they walked deeper into MKT. The constricted space along the path, made worse by cycles carelessly parked around and hawkers squatting down, reminded Abhishek of the lanes in Chandni Chowk which he visited earlier in the day. The crowd was not as dense there but the crammed buildings and the confined surroundings gave the same rigid vibes of being overwhelmed by the environment. Abhishek wondered how everybody there commuted in the narrow lanes, then he realized they must be habituated to those surroundings by then. He on the other hand had the funny feeling of getting clogged in a bottleneck.

That was not to say that MKT lacked beauty, it was quite on the contrary. There was not much of beauty in the old graying buildings. But the Buddhist monastery with its articulate architecture was breath-taking. The sloping roofs of the monastery distinguished by their gentle upward curves at the corners added to the exotic appeal. A few of the prominent shops and restaurants designed their roofs in the 'oriental style' and hung signboards partially inscribed in Tibetan script to become more eye-catching to the crowd.

The restaurant Amit was referring to had a rather bland name, 'Little Tibet,' but Abhishek had to concede it looked pretty. It had the usual oriental styled roof with the curved corners gracing the structure. The main entrance door was decorated with two golden dragons and set under an archway. There were two plaques hanging alongside the wall on either side of the doors. Tibetan inscriptions were scribbled on them though Abhishek could only guess what they could mean. Two marble pillars graced the entrance standing parallel to each other opposite to the doorway. Under the archway was a Chinese lantern shaped like a pumpkin and red in colour. Long frills of coloured paper hung out from the orifice at the bottom.

Amit pushed the heavy wooden doors in and a gust of cold air welcomed them. Abhishek shivered in cold delight as the cold blast of the AC greeted him, he thought he could sense a faint fragrance of cinnamon. The floor was covered in marble and the walls were painted in pastel shades of peach. There were only two windows but both were closed and the curtains were pulled. The cash counter located in the distant right corner looked like a small cabin in itself and even it had its own miniature sloping roof. A small jade dragon adorned the desk. The lighting was dim and soft instrumental music played in the background accentuated by the soft murmur of the guests engaged in conversation. The ambience marveled Abhishek.

"Do you come here often?" he asked Amit.

"You can say that. I used to come here regularly at least once a week when I was a student in the Law Faculty. These days though the visits have been trimmed down due to work fatigue."

"There is this beautiful cinnamon fragrance hanging in the air. I did not know they are fond of using Indian spices in their cooking," Abhishek remarked as the two sat down and Amit laughed loudly. There was a short, curious reaction from other people present but they soon resumed their routine.

"Sorry, I did not mean to embarrass you like this. But the fragrance you are talking about is courtesy a room freshener and is not emanating from the kitchen," Amit explained and called a waiter to serve them two fruit beer, a bowl of Chili Chicken and *Tingmo* (Tibetan steamed bread).

"So how do you rate the day so far?" Amit inquired.

"So far so good, it was an enthralling experience for me to visit Chandni Chowk. Everything they said about the place is true. There is a hint of mystery in MKT as well; it feels so different from the rest of the city. I am glad I came here."

"Something is better than nothing. Slowly and steadily you will graduate to become one of us, now you are still stuck in your private and isolated world."

The waiter soon arrived with a bottle of fruit beer, two beer mugs, a bowl of fried chicken which emitted a fiery aroma, and *Tingmo*. Abhishek gaped at the sight of the *Tingmo*. Initially he thought they were giant-sized dumplings brought to their table by mistake. But as he observed clearly, he discovered that those were actually bun-shaped bread, steamed and ready. Amit took a bite of the chicken and sucked in a quick breath as the pungent flavour burnt his tongue.

Amit took the bottle and poured the beer.

"If only this was the real thing!" Amit joked. "Why do you look so off colour? If I did not know you any better I would have assumed you have fallen in love."

The comment cut into Abhishek. He wanted to subdue his emotions and not speak about Piyushmita but somehow his sentiments spilled out of his mouth.

"Tell me Amit. How do you woo a girl and make her fall in love with you?"

Amit choked on his beer as he heard the words. "That's a surprise. So, you finally started to develop feelings for a girl. Maybe there is still hope for you."

"No, it's not that. I mean leave all that, just tell me how to woo a girl who is so much better than you in every aspect? I feel like a loser in front of her."

"If you feel like that then chances are you will end up like that. How can you expect someone to respect you when you can't respect yourself?"

"I do respect myself!" Abhishek retorted edgily. "It is... it is just that I feel lost in front of her. I want to tell her how I feel but I become numb and words fail me."

"Just gather your confidence and talk to her. Unless she is a telepath she won't know about your feelings for her."
"It's not that I lack confidence. It's just that I am burdened with so much baggage that I am not sure how she will judge me. She might find me a bother."

"Let her be the judge of that. If you presume too much you will only be adding to your anxiety."

"What if she is not interested in me?"

"Find somebody else, simple. Your life will not come to a halt because somebody finds you uninteresting."

"I need her, and I cannot do without her. I feel so strong and confident in her presence; nothing feels impossible to me. I need her to survive; talking to her numbs my pain. I feel like life can still be beautiful for me if she says yes. If only I could go back to my past and do something to change it. That way I would not be suffering from indecision today."

Amit quietly sipped his beer, refusing to participate in this mindless banter. Tired of the words of self-pity, Amit decided to change the subject.

"How do you like the food?"

"Huh? Oh, the food is delicious, especially this bread. But I was surprised to discover that it tastes like any other bread you find in India."

"Bread usually tastes like bread," Amit replied drily.

"No, I mean I was hoping for a little for exotic something."

"Try the chicken, it tastes fantastic and it will distract you from the bread. My mother used to cook chicken like this for me when I was young. It was her favourite dish. The only difference is that the one we are having right now is much spicier. Tell me Abhishek, what dish did your mother love to prepare for you?"

Abhishek froze. A wave of pain washed over him, a forlorn expression etched on his face as old wounds were reopened. He was pushed back to the past he so desperately wanted to forget.

"I don't remember."

"That is funny. You don't even remember your mother's favourite dish?"

"Why are you being so persistent about these things, why should my personal life interest you so much?" Abhishek lashed out without warning. He did not realize it but his sudden outburst drew attention for a brief moment from everyone present.

A long, awkward silence followed but Amit kept his calm. The two finished their meal in an uneasy truce.

Amit asked for the bill and paid the amount. Both of them rose silently and walked towards the exit. It was fifteen minutes past seven in the evening. Dusk was settling in and the blazing afternoon heat was fading away. A couple of shops and stalls had switched on their lights and the pedestrian traffic slightly increased in volume. A few of the old people strolled about in the narrow gullies in their traditional Tibetan attire. In the sunset of their lives the nostalgic attachment for their lost homeland must have become strong and inseparable. Separated from their roots they were trapped in the crossroads, neither here nor there; they were lost in the middle. Yet they continued to wander on the tapered lanes and culverts of a foreign country, perhaps carrying in their heart a faint yet diminishing hope of things being better again. A procession of monks attired in saffron Buddhist robes passed by them presumably towards the monastery. Abhishek envied their ability to keep calm and find inner peace even in their most testing times. It was something he sorely lacked.

"MKT with its Tibetan folk and exotic culture adds a nice touch of cosmopolitan colour to Delhi, don't you think so?" Abhishek opined.

Abhishek was feeling guilty for his flare-up in the restaurant and wanted to make amends. He was upset with the situation but felt helpless to check himself. Childhood had been a trying time in his life when he had been through a lot of emotional upheaval. He still felt uncomfortable talking about the subject. He needed support to break out of his personal quagmire and he was hoping it would be Piyushmita.

"Yes, their presence adds beauty to the demographic structure of this city. Anyways I think we should be going back home now. It had been a long session and we should call it a day. Come, we will get an auto near the main gate of the colony." Amit booked a cab one last time for the day and asked to be dropped at Vijay Nagar, double storey.

From Chandni Chowk in north Delhi to CR Park in south Delhi to back again in north Delhi at MKT it had been a long journey. Abhishek got down at Kingsway Camp near Vishwavidyalaya metro station, he insisted on paying his share of the fare but Amit flatly refused.

"My tour, my expenses." Amit declared.

"Well thank you for the wondrous experience today. I hope we can continue this the next weekend as well. And thanks once again for this souvenir." Abhishek raised the gift-wrapped box.

"You are welcome. Ok, take care and see you later." Amit waved him off.

Abhishek wanted to formally apologize for any rude behaviour from his side. But he was too embarrassed by his conduct to choose the correct words and by the time he could say anything Amit was already gone on his way.

"Next time." he promised himself.

***

CHAPTER – 5

Abhishek began walking back to his PG. In the evening, many groups of college students would come out for a walk, sip tea and hang out for fun. As the dusk was slowly and steadily settling down, he could see flocks of students coming out for the evening. Abhishek had mixed feelings towards the younger breed; he envied their zest for life but also despised their impulsive behaviour. Both extreme traits were alien to him. But as he dwelled on the subject further, he realized that the latter may not be entirely true.

He stopped by at a Paan shop near Outram Lines. The owner of the shop was simply known as *Bhaiyya Ji*, nobody bothered to discover his real name and the pseudonym stuck. *Bhaiyya Ji* was in his mid-seventies but looked like a fifty-year-old and was as fit. If not for the strands of grey hair on his scalp, he would have given the impression of being even younger. His mannerisms and attire were simple; he would always be wearing a white *dhoti* and *kurta* to business. Some claimed that *Bhaiyya Ji* wore the sacred thread of the Brahmin but that was something *Bhaiyya Ji* never confirmed or denied; *Bhaiyya Ji* kept his caste a closely guarded secret. Regardless of the season, he would open his shop at seven in the morning sharp and close down the shutters at eleven in the night. That routine was the same for every day except Sunday when he would open shop at twelve noon. Breakfast, lunch and dinner were delivered by a *dabbawalla*, which *Bhaiyya Ji* had inside his shop. He has been around for longer than people cared to remember and has become a local celebrity of sorts.

Bhaiyya Ji's outlet was one of the more modest shops in size and appearance. It was squeezed between a pharmacy and a retail store, elevated at a height of three feet from the ground and another three feet wide. It was difficult to estimate the length, but, it was suffice, to think that there was enough space for *Bhaiyya Ji* to store his wares. The walls for some inexplicable reason were kept unpainted. A solitary 40-watt incandescent bulb would provide light in the evening, bathing the shop in a ghostly yellow hue that emphasized the shadows as much as it provided luminosity. Naturally there was not enough space for him to stand but such minor details did not bother him much. The whole day he would be sitting cross-legged in a yogi position applying *kattha* and *chuna* to *paan* and handing out cigarettes to the customers along with his never-ending discourse on love, life and practically every topic under the sun.

It was from *Bhaiyya Ji* that Abhishek purchased his first cigarette and got an earful as well.

"Are you lighting a cigarette for the first time *babu*?" *Bhaiyya Ji* asked suspiciously when he saw Abhishek fidgeting with the matches in a futile attempt to light his cigarette.

"No, why would you even think like that? I have smoked before. Now let me light my cigarette in peace." Abhishek tried his best to sound annoyed and continued with his attempts.

The cigarette would light for a brief moment and get extinguished much to his frustration. *Bhaiyya Ji* who was looking all this while with a bemused smile offered help.

"Let me try babu," *Bhaiyya Ji* extended his hand. Left with no options Abhishek handed over the half-burnt cigarette. The experienced old man put the cigarette to his mouth, touched a flame to its tip and let out a puff of smoke.

"Here *babu*, take your cigarette. First you need to put the cigarette to your mouth to light it, merely holding it by your hand and putting the tip to flame seldom works. Don't inhale the first drag too hard or you will have a severe bout of coughing." *Bhaiyya Ji* handed over the lit cigarette to a thoroughly embarrassed Abhishek.

"If I was married and had children, my son would have been of your age *babu*. That's why I dare to advise you, do not smoke. When you light a cigarette, it is your existence which starts to burn, not the stick. As a shopkeeper, selling cigarettes is my way of earning bread and butter, but as a God-fearing person it is my duty to try and correct the habit of youngsters who experiment with tobacco. Rest is their free will, I can only give advice not alter their destiny. If they want to light up their life in smoke, it is their choice. That would be five rupees for the cigarette please."

That happened years ago when Abhishek was still trying to adjust to a new city. A lot of time had passed since then and he had been a regular customer to *Bhaiyya Ji*; amply demonstrating what he thought of the old man's advice.

"Good evening *Bhaiyya Ji*" Abhishek extended his salutations.

"Arre babu! Good evening, good evening" *Bhaiyya Ji* responded, wiping his red tinged palms in a *gamcha*. "How many do you need one or two?"

"Give me just one, no make it two."

"That's a gift you are carrying *babu*, where did you purchase it?"

"I actually got this from my friend, to keep it as a memento."

"I thought you purchased it to gift somebody. But why are you calling it a memento?" There was surprise in *Bhaiyya Ji's* question.

"My stay in Delhi is going to be soon over. In two weeks, I will be leaving this city forever and going home."

"Oh, but you will be missed *babu*. I will miss you a lot. Over the years I have interacted with many people and seen many customers but for me *babu* you will always be special."

Abhishek was pretty sure that the same words would have been used for any random person in his place but he decided to humour the old man.

"Thank you *Bhaiyya Ji* that was very kind of you."

"But *babu*, you have been in Delhi for so many years. Surely you will miss this city and may even feel disappointed over your departure, isn't it true? Ah! I can see it on your face that it is true. I am an old man *babu* and I have seen life, a lot more than you I dare say. Over these years of my existence I have seen nearly every facet destiny can throw at me. Let me give you some parting advice *babu* so that in future you can benefit from it." *Bhaiyya Ji* said rubbing a hand over his balding scalp.

Bhaiyya Ji shifted his position slightly and straightened the crease of his spotless white *kurta*. Sitting cross-legged like a hermit in meditation, his back erect, he placed his palms on one knee each. The glow from the light-bulb behind him gave the illusion of a halo around his head. His gaze was fixed on Abhishek but his eyes seemed to be looking beyond him. *Bhaiyya Ji* gave him the impression of Charles Marlow, the fictional character from Joseph Conrad's cult novella "Heart of Darkness". He cleared his throat and began in a deep solemn voice.

"Life is the biggest mystery in our world *babu*. Nobody knows what a soul is, where it originates from, why we exist and what happens to us after we die. Many great sages and scholars have meditated on the subject over the ages but none could provide a definite answer. Some put forward theories of heaven and hell and some of reincarnation. Yet some are of the opinion that life is nothing but an illusion, as written in our scriptures. I have my own opinion on this subject, *babu*. For me the truth of life is that it is a journey from birth unto death with death being the final reality which we all will have to ultimately accept.

Whatever we earn and accomplish in our lives stays behind us in this mortal realm. We do not carry our wealth and success, or poverty and failure into the afterlife. Everything around us is simply a cipher, a myth. What then is the purpose of our existence?

Why do we live *babu*, simply to draw breath? I humbly believe that we are all here for a specific role to play in the game of destiny. It may look minor to you and me but in the larger scope of things it can have a pivotal effect. Take my case for example, who am I *babu*? I am just a humble old man in his seventies who runs this little shop selling *paan* and cigarettes for a living. Not much of a role if you look at the surface. But *babu*, every day I meet scores of customers. They are from different social backgrounds and everybody has their own unique story. They come to me and share their woes or any tales of interest. Likewise, *babu* I try and help them with their troubles by giving advice on how to deal with various obstacles in life and even indulging in a little gossip at times to keep them in good humour.

God has made me modest, *babu*. I will not boast but I am amongst the most famous personalities in this locality. Every rich person in Kingsway Camp has heard of me. I may be a humble *paanwallah* but I have met countless people over many years of my business. I have listened to their stories, provided help and comfort when needed, motivated them and even set up matrimonial alliances on more than one occasion. This *babu*, I believe, is the reason behind my existence. I live to serve others. Everybody is here in this world for a purpose *babu*; even you have a role to play. You may not know about it right now but you will perform your part assigned to you by destiny.

The second aspect of life is expectations, and the fulfillment or failure of the same. I will not tell a lie *babu*, more often than not, expectations end up in failure. Such is fate. Some accept failure with stoic resilience, some continue to fight back, and yet some willow in dejection and disappointment. No mortal can know what has been ordained for him. I am a humble man and I do not know much about desires but I did tell you that life is a mere illusion. The world that we live in is not the reality; this is not the truth. People are aware of it but they are not ready to accept it. People are easily seduced by the dazzle of the mortal realm. They form intense attachment to things of this world but they forget that these things are transient, just a minor blip in the journey called life. When their time comes, these things will fade away like dew in sunlight. People do not understand this simple truth and as a result they suffer from dejection and disappointment - the two primal reasons for suffering in human kind.

There is no end to human desires *babu*, the ancient scriptures would verify my claims. The human mind craves for possession. Our wants are unlimited and that is solely the reason why they must remain unfulfilled. It is indeed ironic; people get attached so much to things that will not remain with them forever. You carry a burden in your heart. Learn to let go *babu*, when you turn to dust then words like happiness and grief will hold no meaning for you.

Your eyes betray a long-subdued sadness *babu*. You search for something that you have long lost and you seek support doing so. Your quest will become your obsession and before you even realize, you will be caught in the web of expectations. Do not grieve for what you have lost; do not grieve for what cannot be yours. This world is merely a temporary shelter. Life is only transient. Live it, fulfill it, but, do not get lost in its trappings."

By the time *Bhaiyya Ji* was done with his monologue, Abhishek was halfway through his second cigarette. His mind was reeling from the barrage of philosophical mumbo-jumbo that *Bhaiyya Ji* had unleashed. Not a word of the long sermon made an iota of sense to him. The speech sounded more like the bickering of a lonely, frustrated old man. Maybe *Bhaiyya Ji* was pouring out his frustration in front of him or perhaps engaging the customers in long conversations is his marketing ploy for selling more goods. For all he knew, the old man could have been babbling nonsense. Luckily, for him a few other customers had arrived and they initiated a conversation of their own. Abhishek quickly wrapped up his thoughts and bid *Bhaiyya Ji* adieu before the old man got a chance to start again.

***

CHAPTER – 6

Abhishek continued walking towards his PG crossing a multitude of buildings on the way. The area was densely packed, similar to any other locality in Delhi. Other than residential complexes and stores, the locality was also filled up with two hospitals, a primary school, a Gurudwara, a gymnasium, a fruit and vegetable market, the obligatory residential park and even a local slum. Abhishek still remembered the culture shock of seeing so many people and edifices in a crammed colony. Mundane things like personal space were reserved only for the elite upper crust in the city.

He finally reached his residence, a grey coloured three-storey building adjacent to the community park. The ground floor belonged to the landlord Mr. Ashok Mehra and the other floors were rented out as paying guest accommodation. Mr. Mehra and his wife, Mrs. Rita Mehra were in their late sixties, they were regular middle-class Delhi folk where Mrs. Mehra kept herself occupied in watching daily soaps and Mr. Mehra whiled away his time strolling in the park by himself. They did not go out much, except for social occasions like the marriage of their neighbours' kin or religious ceremonies like *Jagran*. Other than these rare occasions, the Mehras do not have much of a social life. Their center of existence was confined to a housing colony in Outram Lines.

The Mehras reportedly have another three-storey building put on rent in Gandhi Vihar, North Campus but Abhishek has never seen it. The Mehras had a child, a son named Jatin, who would be around thirty-four years of age. He had completed his education from Delhi University and gone to the US for higher studies. In the US, he found employment and eventually decided to settle down there. His parents were not too supportive of the idea but

66

they could do precious little. Jatin's communiqué with his family in India was dwindling down every year. He had informed his parents that he had fallen in love with an American girl and he could not afford to return to India at that juncture of his life. One fine evening, the Mehras received a hand-written letter from Jatin informing them that he finally married his lady love. That was the last they had heard from him. It had been six years since they received the letter, there had been no contact with their son ever since.

The PG could house a total of sixteen tenants but it was not always filled to capacity. For some reason the occupants seemed to be moving out after a year, at times even sooner. Competition was tough in the property market where landlords lured businesses with better housing facilities and competitive rates. On average, a person in north campus does not remain in the same PG or apartment for more than two years. Abhishek was the exception, debunking all theories he steadfastly remained in the same PG which provided him with shelter when he had first arrived in the city.

On the way to his room in the second floor, he saw Mr. Mehra showing off the place to a prospective tenant. A couple of beds in the first floor have been vacant for more than a week and Ashok Mehra was showing the same to different clients over the days, that day was no different. Adjusting his horn-rimmed spectacles, he was trying his best to woo the visitor by pitching for and exaggerating the facilities in his PG. There was a sense of urgency in Mr. Mehra's sales pitch and it was enough to understand that he was in need of money.

Abhishek had not informed his landlord about leaving Delhi. Given the current circumstance, he half-expected the old man to raise some degree of tantrum when he would break the news. Abhishek decided to have a chat post-dinner since he did not feel like it was a good time. With a polite nod of his head to the two people present, he continued on his way.

He reached his room in the second floor and opened the door. The room was a simple affair. It was comparatively larger in size than Amit's room but the basic structure remained the same. The room was occupied by two single sized beds, two study tables and their accompanying chairs, two wooden *almirahs* and a full-size mirror.

Unlike Amit's apartment there was no attached kitchen and the resulting space was filled up with a motley of objects ranging from a pair of dumbbells, a pair of boxing gloves (but no punching bag), an ironing table with an old iron on top, an old acoustic guitar, a deflated basketball, a laundry basket half filled with clothes, a shoe rack and a small table where Abhishek kept his drawing kit and related accessories. Except for the small table and drawing kit, all the aforementioned items belonged to his room-mate Raj. Being a fickle minded guy, Raj's interest flirted from body-building to boxing to music, but, he could not last in any field for more than a few days. Most of the items depleted without being used. The basketball was a left-over from his school days when his school-team won a championship, now it's just a showpiece lying around. Abhishek's curiosity was piqued by his room-mate's eccentric habits and he even asked him the reason behind his fluctuating interest levels. There was no straightforward answer. Raj would side-step the question with inane comments like "You live only once, so try everything in life."

At times Abhishek wondered if Raj's words had any merit in them. The boy could not hold his interest in anything for long but it was also true that he had dabbled in diverse fields and was better acquainted on subjects, people had hardly heard about. The fickle-mindedness of Raj also acted as a cushion against emotional turbulence. His parents had a messy divorce when he was a child and he grew up changing cities and schools along the way before settling down in Delhi for his University education and career. Raj never had any roots but that worked to his advantage. His lack of fixation with his surroundings helped him to adapt to new situations and people with relative ease. There was no baggage from the past to bog him down. Raj once tried his hand in relationships; he dated a girl and was later unceremoniously dumped by her. He loitered in depression for a day, drowned his sorrows in whiskey and undeterred he tried dating another girl a week later and was soon dumped again. The unending cycle continued to this day but Raj remained unfazed. Perhaps his fickle-minded outlook gave him the impetus to move forward in life.

Raj was not present in the room at the moment. The absence suited Abhishek just fine because he needed his space and some time to be alone. The day's excursion with Amit was a good way of reliving stress and exploring the city but the fracas in MKT left him with a bitter taste in his mouth.

To relieve his stress, Abhishek logged online in the hopes of finding Piyushmita and spending some time with her. He felt elated to find her present and immediately messaged her. Her response was curt and simple.

"Not now, busy with personal work."

Frustrated at being unable to take control over his life, Abhishek would often break out into a tirade when alone. Goaded by the inner voice, he would scream and abuse himself for being such a failure. At times he would speak out loud trying to analyze the events, what went wrong and how such things could be prevented. There have been instances when confined to his room he would spend hours talking to himself. Abhishek would pretend that there were two people engaged in the conversation when in reality it was him all alone.

Alone in his PG, Abhishek underwent his familiar process of self-flagellation. He cursed himself, loathed the snobbery of Piyushmita and envied Amit's carefree nature. Abhishek went through the process over and over again until his head felt lighter.

Abhishek decided to arrange his stuff so it would be easier for him to pack them later. There were not many clothes to carry back. But the books posed a problem. Abhishek had over two hundred books in his possession. It was too much of a weight to carry along but he could not let go off them. Abhishek would need bigger bags to accommodate them but he was adamant in carrying them back with him.

After all work was done, Abhishek decided to have a chat with the Mehras.

The Mehras did not have a helper in their household. Sixty-year-old, Rita Mehra did all the household chores from cooking to cleaning. The old lady would wake up early in the morning, perform her *Puja* and begin her daily routine. Even in her old age she would take the broom and diligently sweep every nook and corner of the building. More often than not, her dedication towards her work would embarrass the younger boys in the PG who would offer to assist her but Mrs. Mehra would politely refuse their help. Ashok Mehra tried introducing her to the vacuum cleaner to ease her labour but she refused that as well. The only concession she allowed was a washing machine because her hands would go numb with cold doing the laundry in winter. Maybe physical labour was her idea of keeping herself busy and distracted, that's why Mr. Mehra did not interfere too much with his wife's routine.

The steadfast schedule of Mrs. Mehra ensured that kitchen hours was rigid and not to be trifled with. Breakfast was served at seven-thirty in the morning, lunch at twelve noon and dinner at nine in the evening. For working professionals, it was not always possible to adhere to her kitchen time-table but Mrs. Mehra was kind enough to keep the food warm for them. Her only request was that boys having dinner late at night should wash the dishes because she retired to bed early.

Quickly freshening up in the washroom, Abhishek made his way to the dining hall on the ground floor. The hall of the Mehras' three-bedroom residence was partitioned in the middle by a wall of curtain. On one side of the partition was the drawing room and on the other side was the dining hall. The dining hall was a humble affair, a square shaped space with enough room to fit in a dining table that could sit six and a wash basin at the corner. The hall was connected to the kitchen by a small archway. The University students from the first floor had already occupied four of the seats on the table while Mr. Mehra occupied the fifth. The Mehras usually dine together and sat after the guests were done, but in times of extreme anxiety Ashok Mehra joins in whenever he felt like. It was a bit surprising but not unusual.

The menu for the dinner was *dal, rajma* and *roti*. Mrs. Mehra served the food to her husband and other attendees on the table and went back to the kitchen. Mr. Mehra tore a piece of his *roti*, dipped it in the *dal* and munched on it absent-mindedly.

The dinner was a silent affair and the guests left one by one. Abhishek reluctantly had a *roti* and was long done with it. He patiently waited for Mr. Mehra to finish his dinner; the old man was in no hurry though and was lost in his own thoughts. After what seemed like an awfully long time, Ashok Mehra was finally done.

"Mehra uncle, I need to talk something important with you." Abhishek started. There was no response and Abhishek tried again. "Mehra uncle! We need to talk."

"What? When did you come here? Oh, for the dinner I see. But you are already done. You wanted to talk of course, but what do you want to talk?"

"It's about an important matter uncle. I need five minutes from you."

"Five minutes you say? Ok you will get your five minutes. I will give you time but first let me carry my dish to the kitchen."

Abhishek watched as Mr. Mehra fumbled with the plate and bowls before managing to carry them away. Abhishek too followed suit and carried his utensils to the kitchen sink. After washing their hands and having a glass of water each they both returned to the drawing room.

"Yes, my boy, what is it that you want to say?" Mr. Mehra asked. Abhishek noticed the strain and fatigue on the old man's face and almost felt sorry for what he was about to divulge.

71

"Uncle there has been some sort of development in my office." Abhishek began slowly and softly. "They are expanding their business and branching out to different parts of the country. They are opening a branch in Guwahati as well. They need employees who know the region well and are adept at handling local issues. In this regard I have been deputed to Guwahati to manage the business there. In simple words, uncle, I am leaving Delhi. I will be heading to Guwahati in two weeks."

Ashok Mehra was looking at Abhishek all the while and continued doing so without any change in his expressions. After a slight pause he questioned," When are you coming back to Delhi?"

"Uncle, I won't be coming back to Delhi. I am going home forever."

"Yes, go home. You should go home and meet your parents. They have not seen you for so long, they must be worried. They will be happy to see you. But you have not said when you are coming back?"

"I won't be coming back uncle. I have been posted to Guwahati." There was almost a look of apology on Abhishek's face when he reiterated for the third time that he is not coming back to Delhi. He could now imagine why the old man was being so distraught.

"You won't be coming back, as in you are going to leave this PG forever. There will be another vacancy here." Realization finally dawned on Mr. Mehra but it only accentuated his distress. "When are you paying the rent?"

"But the rent for July has already being paid. Last week I cleared my dues with you."
"Yes, yes of course. You had cleared your dues for the month of July, but what about August? You should pay the rent for August as well."

"Uncle I would have surely given you the rent for next month. But

I am leaving in the last week of July, which is this month. Instead I was hoping that you would reimburse the security money I had deposited with you."

Ashok Mehra's body froze in shock when he heard the words. The colour drained off his face.

"What, what do you mean I have to pay you back? Why should I give you my money? I will not give my money to you or anybody else." His palms had balled into fists as he shook with agitation. The eyes were red in defiance.

Abhishek was exasperated and fast losing his cool, but with great restrain he managed to phrase his words. "Uncle I am leaving Delhi on July 27th that is four days before the month ends. I am not even asking you to refund me these four days' money. All I am saying is my claim on the security money I had deposited is justified and I need it."

He hardly finished his sentence when Ashok Mehra's body went into a hysterical fit. The old man's face was distorted by fear and anger in equal measure. Abhishek watched him with growing concern. Mr. Mehra's going through bouts of incoherence was not unusual; it was an open secret in the PG. But Abhishek feared that the old man was turning permanently insane. He was at a loss to handle the situation when fortunately, Mrs. Mehra appeared. She must have overheard the conversation and decided to intervene before things got out of hand.

"Please do not mind him. He has not been keeping well for the past few days. There have been too many vacancies in the PG of late and he has not been able to handle the loss well. I will explain the situation to him once he becomes a bit stable. Please do not worry, I will ensure that you get your money back." Mrs. Mehra pleaded and Abhishek had no option but to relent. He quietly walked back to his room.

Once back in his room, Abhishek dwelt on what had just transpired. He felt he should have taken a more sympathetic approach when dealing with his landlord. The Mehras have been prone to bouts of acute depression for years; in fact, he became aware of their condition on his first year in the PG. The old couple has their own way of coping with their loneliness. While the former would indulge in sporadic outbursts the latter would cork her emotions with a stoic face and while away her grief in silence. Abhishek felt a pang of guilt when he recalled the face of a pleading Mrs. Mehra. Perhaps he should not have been so adamant with his demand for money. Pricked with the needles of a guilty conscience he lit up a cigarette to distract himself.

Abhishek retired to bed early. The next day he woke up at nine in the morning. On Sundays he usually woke up late but that day he was too nervous. Things were changing fast around him and he wanted to keep pace. Abhishek loitered in his room checking if there was anything he missed out while arranging last night, there was none. Raj had not returned yet, so he had the room for himself. After fidgeting for a few minutes, Abhishek made a call to Amit.

"Good morning Amit."

"Good morning."

"I just wanted to know if you are free today"

"Why?"

"If you are free we can go out today. There are other places in Delhi I wanted to visit. Modern places this time, with no baggage of history, so that you don't feel alienated."

"I am sorry but I already have plans for today. There is an informal get together at my client's place today at noon. A few important things about work may come up so I can't afford to give it a miss. I hope you can understand."

"No worries, it's not an issue." Abhishek had his reservations on the truth of Amit's claims but he did not put that down in words.

He absent-mindedly flung his phone to the table where he kept the clay elephant gifted to him the day before by Amit. Memories, Abhishek thought, the silent component that shapes an individual's persona.

Abhishek thought of trying his hand in painting to kill time but his mind was not in the effort. All he could draw was a brush of colours that had no shape or texture but merely crisscrossed each other, giving the impression of something colourful and vibrant on the surface but which otherwise had no meaning. Finding no other means of killing his boredom, Abhishek decided to go out for a walk.

After wandering aimlessly in the street for some time Abhishek decided to retire to his room and sleep further. When he woke up it was three in the afternoon and he was groggy eyed.

Abhishek looked around the room to get his bearings straight. He turned his head full 180 degrees from side to side and nearly jumped in shock when he saw Raj sitting on the chair and watching him with a bemused smile.

"Rise and shine your majesty. It is afternoon now," Raj joked.

"When... when exactly did you come back today?" Abhishek overcame his shock and managed to ask him.

"It's been a while. I met uncle, our landlord, downstairs. He told me that you are leaving Delhi."

"Yes, on the twenty seventh of this month. I had a sort of showdown with him yesterday over the security money I had paid." Abhishek gave a brief summary of the spat between him and Mr. Mehra.

"No wonder he looked sore. But it's good that you demanded your money, you should fight for what is your right."

"I am feeling guilty now. I should not have shouted at the old man like that. They already have enough troubles of their own. I should not have pressed my demands. I have decided to forfeit my security money. It is not a big amount anyway, it won't do me much good but at least it will give the old couple some peace of mind."

"Don't be a sentimental fool. Everybody in this world have problems of their own. We have to face them ourselves; it is foolish to expect help from others. Mr. Mehra may not have sympathized with you the way you are being sympathetic with him. It's good to help others but you should not lose out on yourself in the process."

"Well, I guess that's just me." Abhishek shrugged his shoulders.

"That is up to you to decide. You sleep or get refreshed, whichever you feel like. I have to leave now as I have other things to attend to."

Before Abhishek could say something in reply Raj was gone.

The next two weeks went away in a blur for Abhishek. He kept himself busy in office, there was not much official work to do but he decided to study and gain a proper understanding of the Guwahati market, and potential clients and their requirements. His boss Joseph had told him that he could hire one intern to work under him. Further expansion of the Guwahati office would depend upon how much business it can generate. It was a subtle reminder to Abhishek that the company was expecting him to put up a good show.

Abhishek informed Mr. Mehra about his decision to forfeit the security money much to the latter's delight. The old man wanted to hold Abhishek for tea but he politely refused. There were other important things to do. He had to arrange for transport to carry his bulk luggage to the railway station.

On the morning of July 27, Abhishek was ready for departure. He bid adieu to his room-mate Raj. Raj was not the kind of person who would get emotional but Abhishek sensed that that day might an exception.

"So, Raj, it is finally the time to say goodbye."

"So, it is my friend, so it is." Raj agreed as he gave his departing room-mate a hug in front of the mirror.

On his way downstairs, Abhishek briefly dropped by his landlord's place to bid them adieu. Mr. Mehra was his glum self as usual but Mrs. Mehra was more warm and receptive. She lovingly caressed her hand across his face once.

"Take care, my child. Try and keep in touch if possible." She said in a steady but soft voice.

"Of course, aunty, I will." Abhishek replied. It was a lie but Abhishek hoped the lie will give her some consolation.

The cab took Abhishek to the railway station after negotiating the tense Delhi traffic. Abhishek had an inclination to meet *Bhaiyya Ji* one last time, but when he looked out of the window the old man was not there, in fact the shop was shut down. It was an unusual thing because *Bhaiyya Ji* never broke his routine.

Abhishek hired a coolie to carry his luggage to the coach. The coach attendant was all charm and servitude for the first-class passengers in the Rajdhani. Abhishek paid him a hundred rupees and ordered for a packet of cigarettes. It was technically an illegal thing to do but money has the power to negotiate.

After half an hour the engine let out a sharp whistle, signaling its intent to march on its journey. Abhishek decided to stand near the door and watch the city pass by him. There was a flurry of noise in the platform as the passengers in the other coaches shouted farewell to their friends and relatives on the platform and vice versa. There was nobody for Abhishek to wish him a safe journey, not even Amit. But he did not think too much about it.

77

As the train chugged forward slowly, Abhishek lit a cigarette and glanced up at the sky. It was the final days of July, monsoon had arrived and he could see a few grey clouds gathering together in the possible outbreak of rain. A few minutes later, raindrops started falling down to the Earth; a few of them caressed Abhishek's face on their Earth-bound journey. Abhishek watched, as Delhi, his adopted home for a decade, flashed away before his eyes. The train moved ahead and crossed the Yamuna River, gradually leaving the city behind. He cast one final glance at Delhi and went inside. The next day it would be a new city and a new journey.

*

CHAPTER – 7

After a journey of thirty-eight hours, thanks to unavoidable delays, the train reached its destination in Guwahati at five in the evening. As soon as the train came to a halt, an army of coolies boarded the train and demanded if the passengers required their services. Abhishek hired one coolie and told him to carry his luggage to the taxi stand. The coolie obliged and nearly bent in half under the burden of the excess baggage.

The coolie huffed his way to the nearing stand. Abhishek paid him off, even giving him extra twenty rupees for his trouble. The taxi drivers seeing a potential customer hounded on him and asked where he would like to go. Abhishek apprised them that he needed to be dropped at the Navagraha Hill in Silpukhuri and inquired if anybody was willing to go. Taxi drivers in India, especially those at railway stations and bus stands, are not known to be emphatic with the concerns of the passengers. Guwahati was no exception. Silpukhuri is a mere two kilometers from the station but the drivers charged a king's ransom. Given the luggage and journey fatigue Abhishek had no choice but to give in to the demands.

The taxi made its way towards Silpukhuri crossing the buildings of the Reserve Bank of India, The Public Library and Assam State Museum on the way. Abhishek looked out of the window, in his decade long stay in Delhi he had never visited Guwahati and during his absence the city had changed considerably. Public infrastructure had greatly improved, with the roads getting bigger and better, public transport developed and public edifices getting renovated. Even the number of malls and retail chains increased dramatically signaling a burgeoning middle class with disposable income. But the crowd, vehicular traffic and the accompanying chaos had increased as well.

The locality of Silpukhuri falls in Radha Govinda Baruah Road or simply R.G. Baruah Road. The road named after an eminent personality, hailed as the architect of modern Assam, was arguably the busiest road in the city. Even renewed work on infrastructure failed to check the menace of incessant vehicular traffic on the roads. The situation was further compounded during peak traffic hours. Abhishek was caught in a jam and cursed under his breath, irrespective of how much the city has grown and developed, some things always remain constant. After a stammering ride for thirty minutes, Abhishek finally reached Silpukhuri.

The name Silpukhuri was derived from an eighteenth-century pond constructed under the patronage of the erstwhile Ahom ruler of Assam, Rajeshwar Singha. The word *pukhuri* in Assamese language means pond, and this particular pond derived its name from the stone plaque found on its banks.

The road to Navagraha hill was directly perpendicular to Silpukhuri pond. The actual name of the hill was Chitrasal hill but the name Navagraha stuck because of the Navagraha Mandir, or temple of nine planets, that graced the tip of the hill. The temple was home to nine Shiva lingams where each one represented one of the nine celestial bodies. The Shiva lingams were covered with a coloured garment symbolic to each of the nine planets. A Shiva lingam in the center symbolized the sun. The nine planets were central to Hindu mythology because those celestial bodies were believed to influence and affect the destiny of an individual. The thought brought a dry smile on Abhishek's lips. For years he had been at the receiving end of fate.

Other than the Navagraha temple, the locality was also home to a Hindu crematorium, and a colonial era graveyard which was the final resting place for soldiers who fought for the British Empire in the Second World War. After a circuitous route, the taxi finally reached the destination. The driver was gracious enough to unload the luggage and carry it to the doorstep of his house, but, after paying an exorbitant fare Abhishek expected this much assistance from him. Abhishek stood at the gate and took a long look at the concrete structure that was his home. He felt a sense of fondness for the familiar architecture, but not the memories associated with it.

An austere single storey residence, the house was still the same in appearance as it was all those years when he had left for Delhi. It had been untouched by renovation and any effort on maintenance has been negligible. The walls outside were never painted and the plasters were coming off from more places than he could count. The glass on the window panes was stained with dust, and the roof of corrugated metal sheets covered in rust and in need of urgent repair. There was a garden which had once seen better days but it was then simply an unkempt tangle of thorny shrubs, bush and wild plants haphazardly sprouting all over the place. A few broken earthen flower pots, that once housed rose plants, were the only evidence that the place used to be an aesthetic lawn filled with colours and fragrance. A jujube and a *Krishnasura* (Assamese for *Gulmohar*) tree were the only legitimate plantations in the garden. The jujube had stopped bearing fruit but the tree and its thorns were as sturdy as ever. The *Krishnasura* on the other hand portrayed a different picture. Its trunk was bent and misshapen as a result of neglect and mishandling in its formative years, which gave an unsightly bearing to an otherwise beautiful tree.

Abhishek stood in front of the door and slowly raised his hand to ring the bell. There was no sound of any movement from inside the house nor was any indication given that the door-bell was heard. Exhausted from a long journey Abhishek's impatience got the better of him and he firmly implanted his thumb on the bell giving out a series of rings, only then it elicited a response.

"Yes, yes coming. And I am aware of the chime of my door-bell. You don't have to continuously play it out for me." An irritated and grumpy voice from inside the house shouted.

A moment later the door was opened by his father Arindam Baruah. A man in his mid-sixties, Mr. Baruah was of average height but his broad shoulders and ramrod straight posture was an indicator of a once strong body and the determined personality he still had. There were grey strands of hair on his head as expected of a man his age. Unlike other people Mr. Baruah never bothered to dye his hair, he believed such exercises were done by escapists who wanted to run from the inevitability of old age and death. Mr. Baruah did not have a beard either for he believed that beard and stubble were compensation for a man's lack of masculinity. His eye sockets were marked by crow's feet but his gaze was still alert.

"Young man, when you said you will be arriving today, you ought to have had the sense to inform me of the time the train would reach the station I had to wait for you the whole day and I could not even enjoy my lunch in peace. Still the careless boy! When will you show signs of maturity?" The reproach was unmistakable in his speech.

"Yes, I forgot to mention the expected time of arrival, but you did not remind me either."

"Your father has to do everything for you. For once just try to stand on your feet and make decisions without being prompted by others. What will you do when I am gone?"

The last question was rhetorical and aimed more at Arindam himself than his son but that did not mitigate the effect on the latter. Conversation between father and son were formal at best and non-existent otherwise. There have been episodes when both father and son would stay in the same house without talking for days. There was no overt sense of animosity but it was a bitter truth that there was a conspicuous lack of emotional connection between the two. They rarely, if ever, shared common ground on any matter.

Abhishek could feel a familiar sense of frustration creeping in him due to his father's overly patronizing attitude. But he did not wanted things to deteriorate on the first day of arrival to his house after a gap of many years. He quietly walked inside towing his luggage behind him.

The house had two bedrooms, a hall and a kitchen. The hall and the rooms were not too spacious to accommodate people and hold large social gatherings but guests at their house had always been a rare occurrence. The interiors of the house were painted in lively colours of green and light blue but the colours have long since faded. Abhishek's room was small and narrow in dimension, resembling the shape of a shoe box if viewed from top. It contained his bed, a wooden *almirah* and a study table and chair that he used when he was a school student.

Mr. Baruah does not usually enter the room of his son, but there were tell-tale signs that the room was tidied up; as evident by the lack of dust on the floor and the table of an otherwise unused room. The bed sheet and curtains that adorned the windows were fresh. Abhishek lazily dumped his luggage wherever he found some free space, pulled his shoes and lied down on the bed closing his eyes and tried to kill the exhaustion.

Abhishek did not realize when he had gone off to sleep but he woke up when the pressure cooker gave a loud whistle. He stared up at the ceiling and caught sight of the dream-catcher swaying gently in the evening breeze.

His father was in the kitchen preparing dinner. Abhishek reluctantly pulled himself out of the bed. He went to the washroom to wash off his sleep by applying water on his face and changed his attire into a pair of boxers and T-shirt. In the meantime, Arindam was done with his cooking; it was a simple affair of rice, *dal*, dry vegetables and salad. His father was already seated on the dining table and about to start with his dinner. Abhishek decided to let him finish his dinner first and switched on the television, randomly flipping through the channels. After a few minutes Arindam was done with his dinner. He carried off the plates in his burly, outsized hands; the scarred knuckles were a grim reminder of his hard past. Abhishek quietly went to the kitchen, got himself a plate and began his dinner. Both father and son like to have their dinner alone and the habit had remained even after all these years. Abhishek soon finished his dinner, washed the dishes and hurried off to bed. In spite of the void and detachment he harboured towards his house, he liked the comfort of his bed. Abhishek closed his eyes as he went off to sleep.

The next morning, when Abhishek woke up, the sight of an unfamiliar ceiling momentarily unsettled him. It took him a minute to realize that he woke up at his home in Guwahati instead of his PG in Delhi. Abhishek wearily realized that he had been away from home for too long. After freshening up he went to the dining table for his breakfast. Mr. Baruah by habit was an early riser and, as expected, he had finished his breakfast earlier and was in the veranda going through the newspaper for the second time. He made no acknowledgement of the presence of his son and neither did Abhishek go out of his way to greet him. He quietly had his breakfast.

***

Abhishek gazed out of the window from his room. Dusk has slowly settled in and the sky turned a hue of light purple brushed with shades of orange on the clouds. The musk smell of the damp earth tickled his nostrils. He had been lying in his house the whole day and he started to get fidgety. Abhishek longed to go outside. He changed into a pair of pyjamas and a loose-fitting cotton T-shirt, put on his sandals and decided to go for an evening walk.

"I am going out for a walk." He called out to his father who was busy surfing the channels on the TV. There was no response and Abhishek did not bother to wait for one.

Abhishek welcomed the gust of the cool evening breeze, it invigorated him. Rains were always full during that time of the year and he could feel the monsoon in the air. He was tempted to pay a visit to the Navagraha Temple but religious devotion had quit him a long time ago and he was already familiar with its architecture. Instead, he continued to walk up the long winding path up the hill until he reached the summit. He sat down and rested on a small mound and looked down at the city below him. As the darkness around him grew steadily he could see a flicker of lights turn on in some of the residential complexes far below.

The city of Guwahati was garrisoned by a garland of hills which provided it a natural barricade against external aggression. The hills provided successful defence of the city against foreign invasion for centuries but at times Abhishek felt that the hills also gave a sense of confinement. Much of Guwahati had changed since he last left. The city had undeniably grown in size; the towering residential complexes were visual proof of that. Abhishek tried to locate the vacant playing ground in the distance where he used to watch boys play soccer and cricket. The vacant ground had long vanished, now gobbled up by a posh shopping mall. Old landmarks and buildings that once dotted the landscape below had been obliterated to make way for new constructions. Change, he reckoned, was not always a gentle procedure.

As more and more lights lit up in the buildings, he noticed the vast swathes of darkness that engulfed them. He strained to see, and observed very faint glows emanating from there. It took him a moment to realize that the darkness was inhabited by slums. The rapid growth of Guwahati had attracted people from all corners of the state and even beyond. But not everybody was well off or fortunate in that fast-evolving city. Many prospered, but many more were now reduced to an existence in slums far away from their native villages, and the comfort of their homes they had left behind. *Reorganizing an entity always brings two facets with it, the good and the bad.* His city was no different.

The night crept in stealthily and the stars were visible on the horizon. Abhishek stared down at the spark of electric lights that lit up the complexes and the faint glow of oil lamps and candles that complimented them. Both seemed to exist in mutual, if uneasy, co-habitation with none eclipsing the other. Abhishek continued to stare as if in a trance at the lines of light that crisscrossed the ground below. He did not realize how long he had been sitting there but soon he felt the chill in the air which made him go cold. He got up and made his way back home.

*** *

The alarm from the table clock rang incessantly and woke Abhishek from his slumber. With a lazy effort he managed to raise his arm and shut down the alarm. Abhishek hated to be woken up so early but he had no other choice. He has to resume his professional duties that day and needed to start early. He received a call last night from his boss Joseph reminding him about the importance of the duties in Guwahati branch for the growth of their company in the region. Abhishek sighed. He could have done with a couple more off days but work was work.

There was no metro in Guwahati and neither did Abhishek own a personal vehicle. He would need to take the bus to commute to office and back. He did not like the idea too much but he had to get used to it. Abhishek waited patiently at the Silpukhuri bus stand and glanced around. A sizeable crowd was present there all eagerly waiting, but the maddening rush that was tangible in the Delhi metro stations was mercifully absent here.

After a few minutes wait, Abhishek found a vacant enough bus to drop him to his office in Ganeshguri. The place got its name from the prominent Ganesh Temple located in its southern part. Many commercial and state administrative offices were sited there. Ganeshguri was situated in the capital complex of Guwahati and for years it had been the prominent market and landmark of the city.

As the years progressed, new markets, bigger and better in size, have overtaken Ganeshguri but the latter was still the symbolic heart of the city; always crowded, active and jostling with life. Due to the incessant chain of vehicular traffic it took much longer than expected for him to reach his destination. The wider roads invited more vehicles and instead of providing relief, it only seemed to have only added to the woes of the commuters. Abhishek wryly wondered if the earlier narrow roads were a better option. He did not have to dwell much on it though as the bus soon halted at the Ganeshguri stand.

Abhishek got down from the bus and made his way to the office. His office was located in one of the outer by-lanes of the market. There was a beehive of buildings already constructed or under-construction that had been fully dedicated to be rented out as office space. A few of the vacant floors would be rented out to cafeterias' and other such business but the majority of the space was reserved for the offices of the newly emerging corporate sector in the region. Joseph Anand had him repeatedly note down the address of his new office. Sternly reminding him that there were no signboards affixed anywhere but that could not be accepted as an excuse for reaching late for work. Abhishek sighed, Delhi or Guwahati, some things never changed. Bosses were always insufferable.

By the grace of God, Abhishek did not have much of a difficulty in locating his address. His office was located in the third floor of a newly constructed building, a fifteen-minute walk from the local bus-stand. There was an elevator but the power connection was yet to be fixed. Abhishek grunted and decided to take the stairs.

His new office was simple yet aesthetically furnished. It was small in its dimensions but there was more than enough space to accommodate all the four employees. There were no windows but a door at the back led to a small balcony which gave access to fresh air and sunlight. The office had an inventory of two computers, the server, a printer, fax machine and a telephone. There was no Photostat machine as yet but Joseph had promised that they would be getting one very soon. A small kitchenette and a washroom were the complimentary luxuries provided by the parent company. Joseph had assured him that as the business would grow they would be hiring more employees and relocating to a bigger office. It was Joseph's style of offering an incentive.

An old man named Chandra Das looked after the cleaning, cooking, and even mundane duties like getting hold of printing paper, paper clips, markers and other stationery items. Chandra was also the go-to man to get photocopies done, booking of parcels and get tea, *samosa* and other snacks from nearby restaurants. Abhishek was bemused by the size of Chandra's portfolio. But what fascinated him was the striking resemblance between Chandra and *Bhaiyya Ji* in their physical appearance. From a distance it would be hard to distinguish between the two.

Another youth named Bokul Medhi, an ordinary looking guy with an odd pair of green eyes, was the system administrator. It was his job to keep the computers running smooth and safe, ensuring database security and protection against any form of malware. But it was the third person in the room that caught Abhishek's attention; a lean, gawky youth much younger than himself and who looked obviously nervous. Abhishek got to know that his name was Pulakesh Bora and he was the intern assigned to work under him. There was anxiety on the boy's face but there was also a stoic determination in his eyes.

"Hi Pulakesh, my name is Abhishek. It is nice to have you in our team."

"Thank you, sir! I will do my best and won't let you down." Pulakesh regrouped his confidence.

"Just call me Abhishek. Are you familiar with your work?"

"A little, but I am a fast learner."

Abhishek discussed the nuances of the job for his young intern. The boy was nervous and made a few mistakes but otherwise he was true to his word of being a fast learner.

***

There was no concession in terms of work for Abhishek and his team. Abhishek had to set up communication with Delhi, apprise them of the details in the office, give a report on the market in the region, prepare a list of prospective clients, collect data on newspapers, electronic media and other platform for advertisements and prepare the 'pitch' for potential clients. Pulakesh was busy assisting Abhishek, who was impressed to see him learn things quickly. Chandra was running various errands like making tea, getting packet of cigarettes from below and other such tasks. The only person sitting relaxed was Bokul, but Abhishek did not have time to envy him.

Abhishek would come home late, exhausted but satisfied. Being busy, kept him away and distracted from issues at home. He was

88

having anxiety about staying under the same roof with his father. Their relationship had always been slippery. He was perplexed by his father's behaviour. When he was in Delhi, his father had informed him that he was not keeping well and frequently asked if he could take a transfer to Guwahati. On coming home, Abhishek realized that his father was perfectly fine. He was relieved to see him in good shape but he could not understand why he had to lie to him. When he would return from office Arindam would just look at him, there were no queries about his work.

A week had passed since Abhishek started working in Guwahati. The expected teething problems were being sorted out and the team was getting into the groove. Business had been forthcoming and it was enough to keep his boss Joseph in good humour, for the time being. It was after a week that Abhishek found time to connect to social media. Piyushmita was online and she sent him a message.

"How are you doing?"

"I am good. I was busy at the new office in Guwahati but I am getting a hang of it now."

"You have moved to Guwahati, when?"

"It's been a few days."

"You could have informed me at least."

"I tried to, but you were busy with personal work."

There was a brief pause at the other end.

"I am sorry, I know I come across rude at times but that is not the real me. I have to leave now but I hope you will keep in touch. Bye."

For the first time in Guwahati, Abhishek experienced a sense of elation. He longed to earn the respect and attention of Piyushmita and he now felt like he was inching closer towards his goal. He was aiming for the stars but Abhishek was undeterred.

***

As the days progressed, Abhishek took more interest in his work. Being placed in charge, there was no boss to constantly keep interfering and finding mistakes. He had full autonomy to conduct his operations. It was a new-found freedom which he loved and he delivered the desired results. Even Joseph applauded the effort and in a rare move sent the team a congratulatory note.

Abhishek did not believe in co-incidences but he considered that all these positive changes in his life had taken place after meeting Piyushmita. He was now sure that the girl was his lucky charm and the necessary support he needed to grow and prosper.

Abhishek wondered if Pulakesh also sought inspiration from his love. The young intern was an introvert and mostly kept to himself. In many ways, Pulakesh reminded Abhishek of himself. He was tempted to ask him but then he thought the better of it. Being the senior, it would not be appropriate for him to pry in the personal lives of his junior colleagues. Abhishek concluded that Pulakesh possibly did not have anybody special in his life; the latter was far too stoic and comfortable in his own space.

***

CHAPTER-8

August had come to an end and it was the early days of September. Piyushmita had thawed her stance towards Abhishek. The two would occasionally meet online where they would have a casual conversation.

Abhishek was in seventh heaven. For all practical purposes he believed that he was living in a dream. He was sure that putting forward a proposal to his love interest was only a formality; she was also infatuated with him. Piyushmita had herself confessed that she found it comfortable to speak on certain subjects with him which she would never bring up in front of others. The other day she was telling Abhishek about an incident that took place with her online. One of her casual friend had put up a funny comment on a photo she had uploaded. Abhishek had seen the photograph; in it Piyushmita was leaning against a wall dressed in skin-tight denims and a low-cut top. Her svelte figure was beautifully highlighted by her attire.

The comment posted by her ex-acquaintance was "Nice melons."

Piyushmita was not the one to take things lying down. She replied, "If you are so jealous of them you should try growing a pair yourself."

The girl did not react to provocation in wild fury; instead her actions were cold and precise. She was a strong character and Abhishek believed she could act as the perfect shield for him. Abhishek could not explain to himself why he was obsessed with her. He felt inclined to believe that a confident girl protecting him was what it would take to fix his life and put him back on track. He needed her love more than anybody else.

*

Arindam Baruah was worried about his son's late-night shifts and he made that clear one day.

"You have been coming home late these days."

"Work dad, a lot of work has to be done."

"I have also worked in my time. But you have been coming home past ten o'clock regularly of late."

"The main office in Delhi is happy with our progress but they also want to maintain the lead and grab as much business as possible while we are going hot. So, I have to stay back late." Abhishek was tired and did not want an argument with his father at that hour.

"I was just worried if you have been eating properly. You did not have your dinner for the past few days. You should look after your health." Arindam shared his concern with his son.

Abhishek was taken aback. His father, as far as he knew, was not an emotional man. In fact, if there was one thing that he was sure his father hated, it was emotions. Abhishek could not remember the last time his father gave into that weakness, as the latter termed it, but something inside him stirred up.

"You worry too much," Abhishek replied gently, "I am looking after myself quiet well and taking my meals at regular hours. I missed dinner on a couple of occasions but I am still keeping healthy." Abhishek managed a smiled at the last sentence.

Mr. Baruah listened without any change in his expression but Abhishek thought he could detect a glow in his father's eyes. He quickly changed his clothes, washed his clothes and went to the kitchen. Dinner was kept ready for him in the hot case. He took a plate and headed towards the dining table. As he chewed on the food he made a mental note to henceforth have dinner at home.

The next morning as Abhishek was about to leave for office his father called out.

"Do you need anything?"

"Why?"

"I just thought it would be nice to ask."

"Thanks, but I don't need anything."

Abhishek was puzzled at his father's behaviour but he did not express his thoughts aloud. It was only when he boarded the bus that he realized the next day was his birthday. Off late his father had been trying to amend for the past by warming up to him. That put Abhishek in a moral dilemma. He had grown up under his father's notorious temper and he had adjusted to life without a word of kindness from him. Seeing a soft and emotional side of his scary father put him in an awkward position. That change in his father should have come years ago, the situation felt awkward for Abhishek but deep within, he was also glad for his father's affection.

Abhishek could not concentrate on work that day. His mind was distracted with all the changes taking place around him. He deputed all his work on Pulakesh while he himself wasted time on social media. He wanted to spend time online with Piyushmita but she was not there. Abhishek left a message for her saying how much he missed her. Unable to focus on his duties Abhishek took a half-day and left.

Arindam was surprised to see his son home so early. He wanted to talk to his son and ask about his life. His own son had been a stranger to him for so many years. Arindam wanted to bridge the gap but he was apprehensive that any wrong move on his part would upset his son. Abhishek greeted his father with a half-hearted smile. He quickly changed his clothing and freshened up. Dinner was served early and for the first time after many years both father and son shared the dining table.

***

After dinner, Abhishek retired to bed early. He must have been sleeping for two hours when the cell phone started rang loudly. Awake and annoyed at the sudden din, he checked the number on the screen but could not recognize it.

"Hello?" Abhishek spoke in barely concealed irritation.

"What did you mean when you said you are missing me?" A deep and commanding female voice demanded on the other end.

"Who is this?"

"Piyushmita"

"Piyushmita!" Abhishek jumped out of his bed in one swift motion. "But how did you get my number?"

"You shared it with me online. Don't you remember?"

"I am so sorry, but surprisingly I don't remember giving you my number."

"Never mind that, tell me what did you mean by saying you miss me."

"Just... just that it's... it's been a while since you have been online. I missed your presence and... and talking to you. That's all." Abhishek managed to stammer a response.

"Is that all?"

"Yes, I swear."

"Fine then."

"I thought you called me for some other reason."

"How did you guess that?"

"What is there to guess? It is past mid-night. Today is my birthday."

"Shit! I did not know about that. My apologies, and wishing you many happy returns of the day."

"Thank you so much! You are the first one to wish me on my birthday. And I feel so..."

"Leave all that for the moment. There is an important thing I need to ask. Do you know a guy named Amit Baishya?"

"I do, he is my ex-classmate. But why are you asking me about him?"

"Leave it, it's not that important. I was busy with something and so couldn't call you earlier. Sorry for disturbing you at this late hour. Goodnight."

"Goodnight."

Confused by her erratic behaviour Abhishek dozed off to sleep.

***

Abhishek should have been in a euphoric mood on his birthday but his present state of mind was far from that. He had to attend office and last night's conversation with Piyushmita had left him puzzled. Abhishek entrusted all the important work to an inexperienced Pulakesh, who was flabbergasted but did not challenge the orders of his senior. Abhishek meanwhile went out to the balcony for a smoke. He had barely dragged two puffs when he got a call on his cell phone; once again it was an unknown number.

"Wishing you a very happy birthday Abhishek."

"Amit?"

"Damn! I knew you would recognize my voice."

"It's so good to hear your voice. I thought you are upset with me or something."

"Why should I be upset with you?"

"We did not part on a positive note last time. I was afraid my behaviour hurt you."

"We never parted and I am always there for you. I am sorry I wasn't there for you at the station when you left, but be rest assured I prayed for your safe journey."

"Thanks, but there is something I need to ask you. How do you know Piyushmita?"

"What made you ask this question?"

"Just answer me, how did you meet her?"

"She is quite a popular character in social circles. A lot of people know her and have heard about her. I happened to chance upon her social media profile and left her a message. But why did you ask?"

"She is one of my online friends. She called me up last night and inquired about you."

"Your name must have cropped up as a mutual friend and she decided to call you. But it is interesting to note that she called you up at night to inquire about me, very interesting."

"What are you hinting at?" Abhishek suddenly grew apprehensive.

"You don't worry about that. You relax and enjoy your birthday. So long, my friend." Amit hung up on Abhishek after breaking into his typical laughter.

Abhishek had a bad feeling about Amit's intentions. Amit was a self-confessed womanizer who enjoyed the company of women. It was possible that Amit harboured similar ambitions about Piyushmita and it was something Abhishek could not tolerate. Abhishek decided to warn her.

***

CHAPTER-9

The days progressed as September gave way to October. Autumn was at the doorstep and the trees already looked bleak, even the setting sun appeared mournful on the horizon. Abhishek prayed that these signs were not an indication of things to come.

There was no contact from either Amit or Piyushmita for the past few days and he hoped that his warning had the desired effect on her. The unexpected hiccup from Amit was putting a strain in his professional work. Caught up in his worries Abhishek would constantly keep delegating important work to Pulakesh much to the young intern's chagrin. Joseph sent repeated reminders to Abhishek to take charge but it all fell on deaf ears. Abhishek decided he had other priorities to attend to.

Abhishek could not devote time to his re-discovered love for painting. He tried his hand in Delhi but left it incomplete. Having jettisoned all cares of responsibility Abhishek decided to try afresh in Guwahati. To his surprise he found the work extremely difficult. As the painting progressed it required more complicated mixture of colours and skilled hand work. It was like Abhishek never had any prior knowledge of art before. Nonetheless he was determined to finish what he had started.

Arindam noticed that his son would come home early from office and lock himself up in his room for hours. He did not dare enter his son's domain but he hoped that his boy knew what he was doing.

***

One evening when Abhishek was engrossed in his painting he got a call from Piyushmita.

"Why are you leaving such funny messages in my inbox?" Her voice was terse.

"I did not do any such thing."

"Yes, you did."

"I only tried to warn you about Amit."

"That was not all you sent. Your friend Amit is a jerk and his comments are even creepier. You two friends make a fine pair."

"Did you reply to his comments?"

"I don't have time for his nonsense."

"Thank God!"

"What do you mean?"

"I was just feeling insecure."

"Excuse me?"

"I was worried about you. Amit has the art of charming people."

"You don't need to worry about me. I can look after myself. I called you to let you know that if you are in touch with Amit tell him I don't find his jokes funny."

"I will let him know if I get in touch with him next time around."

Without any further words Piyushmita disconnected the call. Abhishek was puzzled by her reaction. At one point of time it looked like Piyushmita was warming up to him but now things were going back to how they started. To add to his woes, things in his professional life were quickly turning sour. His laid-back attitude was noticed by Delhi office and Joseph was infuriated. To this effect, one day he got a phone call from the boss himself.

"What is wrong with you Abhishek?" Joseph barked from the other end.

"I beg your pardon sir."

"You are right you do! I have been getting complaints about your irresponsible attitude. I was impressed with your initial work but now I have come to know you are shirking away from your duties and putting the burden of work on a young intern who is still new to the work."

"He is a fast learner sir."

"That is not the point Abhishek." Joseph exploded with rage. "It is providence that the young kid is somehow able to handle the responsibility you have imposed upon him. What I demand to know is why are you being such an escapist? You are the man in charge, not him. If you find yourself incompetent then say it upfront. I will make the intern, the head of Guwahati branch."

"I am trapped in some serious personal issues sir. I am not able to devote my attention to work as I should. For that reason, I am trusting on Pulakesh."

"Utter nonsense! And I am hearing some funny things about you. It has been brought to my notice that you arrive late to office but leave early. And people have seen your hands dabbed in paint. What is going on?"

"I am working on a painting sir, it's something I used to do as a child but could not pursue."

"I don't pay you salary so that you make art." The indignation in Joseph's voice made it clear that he would have loved to personally wring the neck of Abhishek if it was possible. "This is your final warning, disappoint me one more time and you have had it."

The conversation jaded Abhishek and he was bristling from the attack. Pushed into a corner he started cursing loudly accusing everybody including himself for the current mess. For him everybody in the office, and Amit and Piyushmita were conspiring his downfall. Seeing his manic state of mind, Pulakesh sought the company of Bokul as a safety measure. Only Chandra stared at him sympathetically with profound sadness in his eyes as if he was anticipating the inevitable.

Frustrated with everything, Abhishek decided to leave office early as usual. It was in direct violation of Joseph's latest outburst but he was beyond caring.

***

The weather outside was unexpectedly pleasant. A short burst of drizzle from a late-monsoon shower had cheered up the atmosphere. The cool breeze of the rain was soothing, the rich fragrance of rain-soaked earth tickled his senses, the birds were singing out their pleasure and the advent of sunshine against the shower formed a rainbow on the horizon. It was the perfect setting for a Sunday afternoon but Abhishek, busy with a paint-brush in his hand, had no time to reflect upon the beauty around him.

A few days back Joseph verbally destroyed him for his lack of responsibility. Joseph's tirade had the opposite effect. Far from taking control of his duties Abhishek found himself sinking faster in his personal quick-sand. He tried to seek solace in his art but even that seemed to be mocking his current state of affairs. The supposed painting was getting more difficult for him because even he was not sure of what exactly he was trying to create. He thought everything would fall automatically in place once he picked up the brush, but then he found his creativity deserting him. Abhishek considered that his art was too grim and he needed to add bright colours in it to balance the illustration. Yet, no matter how much colour he added, it all merged to create a dark and grotesque image.

To his utter frustration, his intense exertion was not yielding the desired results. He sought inspiration from the thoughts of Piyushmita, but it only antagonized him further. The girl apparently had no consideration for his feelings. Every time she talked to him it had something to do with Amit.

Amit had an irresistible charm about him that people found impossible to ignore. His charisma was his main weapon for being a popular figure in his school days. He was everything the rest of the boys wanted to be. It was a deep-rooted fear in Abhishek's mind that if Amit remained present in Piyushmita's consciousness, things won't go down well for him. An array of thoughts brewed in his mind on how to get rid of this situation. Some of them were benign ones like directly approaching Amit and requesting him to keep away from the woman who meant so much to Abhishek. Rest were darker thoughts which bordered on outright violence. Thoughts of physically intimidating Amit and even getting permanently rid of him crossed his mind more than once. For a moment, even Abhishek felt disgusted at his chain of thoughts. But the inner voice, the one he had known since childhood, was slyly persuading him to keep all options on the table.

***

Abhishek kept a constant vigil on the social media profiles of Piyushmita and Amit to detect any signs of growing proximity between the two. So far things had been satisfactory but Amit did not want to drop his guard. He would send constant messages to Piyushmita's inbox and her cell phone and in the pretext of trying to initiate a casual conversation he would try to gauge her sentiments. It was a hopeless endeavour but even her occasional outbursts could not deter him. That obsessive mania of Abhishek was wreaking havoc on his personal and professional life but he had crossed the point of no return.

During his stint of espionage on Piyushmita's social media profile, Abhishek got to know about her birthday. Armed with the latest information he took upon the task of being the first to wish her. On the professional front, everything about Abhishek was a mess. In blatant disregard of Joseph's commands, he continued to throw responsibility on the young intern. Abhishek had changed his phone number and warned the office not to leak any report of his discrepancies to Joseph.

The night before Piyushmita's birthday Abhishek forfeited his dinner and instead locked himself in his room. Phone in hand, he impatiently waited for the clock to strike midnight. When the clock struck, Abhishek did not lose a second and immediately dialed her number. Much to his disappointment he found her number engaged. He could not believe that on her birthday she was willing to talk to other people instead of waiting for him. Abhishek kept on persisting but to no avail. Either the network would be busy or Piyushmita would be engaged in a conversation with somebody else. When he finally relented in his efforts it showed three past midnight on the clock.

***

Frustrated at things not going his way, Abhishek sulked for a week. He called in sick to office and refused to come out of his room. Arindam was worried by his son's eccentric behaviour but he had seen it all beforehand. He decided that time was the best medicine for his son.

In the week of self-pity Abhishek had severed all connections with the outside world. His phone was switched off, he did not bother to connect online and even work on his obscure painting was put on hold.

When Abhishek regained his composure, he wanted to update himself on information about the world which had snubbed him. He logged onto the internet and checked Piyushmita's social media profile. Abhishek immediately felt like he was cruelly punched in the stomach. Her profile page was *chock-a-bloc* with photographs of her birthday celebrations and an overwhelming majority of them featured his nemesis Amit.

In the photographs Piyushmita and Amit were holding hands and looking deep into each other's eyes. There was a sizeable crowd in the background, who Abhishek deduced would be Piyushmita's

103

friends and well-wishers, looked on admiringly at the couple. A couple of photographs showed the couple holding hands and dancing away with gay abandon and in the other Piyushmita had converted a soft drink bottle into an ad hoc microphone and apparently singing out to Amit. In both these cases, the crowd of onlookers was pictured cheering and applauding the two. Abhishek could sense his age-old unease of people creep back in his soul; crowds always meant trouble for him.

There was a caption to the photo album uploaded by Piyushmita, it read – *I finally found my match*. Abhishek knew well what those words meant. He was not even surprised at what he discovered because he knew that fate had a habit of playing pranks on him. The only thing he found hard to believe was that it took fate that long to pull that latest joke on his life.

Destiny had charted a tough course for his life and Abhishek has always being at the receiving end of it. For years he had suffered misery in silence. But that time, for a brief moment, he had tasted the joys of life thanks to a girl. A stubborn attitude inside him refused to die. He had been a puppet at the hands of fate for too long. That moment, Abhishek was determined to challenge his destiny and he was not willing to go down without a fight.

***

CHAPTER-10

The following day, an unpleasant surprise awaited Abhishek in his office in the form of his boss, Joseph Anand. The man was in a foul mood and the target of his ire was Abhishek.

"So, the genius of Guwahati finally decides to grace us with his appearance." Sarcasm dripped from every word spoken by Joseph. "What time is it showing on your watch now?"

"It's eleven o'clock sir."

"You bet it is." Joseph growled. "And what time were you supposed to be here?"

"I have not been keeping well for the past few days, and that's why I had called in sick and missed office last week. Even now I am not feeling well but my devotion to duty pulled me here." Abhishek pleaded his case.

"*Devotion to duty*, my ass! Don't think I am not aware of your shenanigans. I will have to deal with you but later, I have personally come here to Guwahati for an important meeting with a prospective client because I cannot trust you anymore. I am taking Pulakesh with me in your stead. You stay in office and give me a report on all the work that has been done. I want it printed on paper once I return. I will be back in two hours so you better hurry."

Visibly chastised by the rebuke of his boss, Abhishek sat down to work. His attention span lasted for fifteen minutes before he was engulfed by his personal demons. The more he tried to focus on work, the more his mind would bring up the topic of Amit and

Piyushmita's relationship. In the ensuing tug of war, it was his emotional anxiety which prevailed over him. Setting aside all work Abhishek logged on to the social media to stalk Piyushmita's profile. By a stroke of luck Piyushmita was online and Abhishek decided to directly raise the issue with her.

"Do you have a few minutes to spare? I have something very urgent to discuss with you." Abhishek begged of her.

"Make it quick, I have a lot of work to do."

"When will you stop assaulting me with your insufferable attitude? Every time I try to approach you, you search for ways to put me down."

"Ok fine, don't be so melodramatic. Tell me what it is. "

"Did you personally meet Amit?"

"Yes. I had invited him to my birthday bash and it turned out to be wonderful."

"After all the things you told me about him?"

"I know, it sounds funny right? We started chatting online, and then he called me up on my birthday, things worked out between us and we somehow clicked. He is an extraordinary guy."

"No, he is not an extraordinary guy. He is a debauched pervert and it is not good for you to be with him. Get rid of Amit and keep your distance. That guy is bad news."

"The day I feel like I need the advice of a random stranger I will let you know."

"I am not a stranger! Don't ever call me that again. You don't know how deeply I love you and how much you mean to me. I am grovelling for your attention, for one kind word from you and all you can spare me is your heartless attitude. My life has always been a mess; I have known nothing but pain all my existence. You don't know how many painful memories I have to live with every day. I did not believe I could be happy in my life until I met you. Your presence, even if only virtual, fills me with happiness. You have inspired me to live again and believe in myself. I need your love and support more than anybody else in this world. I am the right guy for you, not Amit. Amit is a ruthless womanizer who can't treasure your importance in his life. Please don't go with him, I need you more."

"Fuck Off."

Those two crude and unexpected words stabbed Abhishek to the core. He thought it was a joke or a message intended for another which accidentally reached him. But a minute later he realized that he could not send any more messages to Piyushmita because she had blocked him. He tried and tried some more but could not reach her. The shock of what just happened made Abhishek explode in nervous laughter before he broke off into a string of expletives attacking everyone within earshot and all those who had been in his life. He continued with his outburst until he felt like his head was splitting apart in pain. Tired, exhausted and broken down, Abhishek headed to the balcony for a smoke.

From the balcony Abhishek looked down in the distance as the smoke from the burning cigarette wrapped around his head further compounding his thoughts. He was lost in his grief when he felt that the radiance of the afternoon sun was diminishing and becoming faint in the distant horizon. At a distance far away from where he was standing, Abhishek watched benumbed as the bright sunlight was overshadowed by a sepia-toned hue. The buildings were now fewer in number and shorter in stature, while many others receded into oblivion revealing vast empty tracts of land like it was many years ago. The sprawling market was shrinking in size before his eyes and the dense crowd was becoming sparse. Wide roads gave way to narrow streets that are more filled with pedestrians instead of vehicles. Abhishek recognized the view, he is now looking at Ganeshguri the way it was over two decades ago.

In the bustling crowd, Abhishek thought he spotted a familiar figure. A lone woman was trying to console her child who was weeping piteously over a cone of ice cream he had spilled on the street. The woman was gently wiping away the tears of the child and whispered soothing words to him. The boy responded to her gentle touch and subsequently calmed down. There was something oddly familiar about the boy and Abhishek realized with a start that he was looking at his childhood self. He recognized the woman and immediately he felt his eyes burn as a warm streak ran down his cheek. It had been ages since he had seen his mother and Abhishek struggled to subdue his sobs. His ears ached to hear her kind words and his fingers longed to touch her loving hands that were wiping off the tears from his face.

Abhishek was lost in his mother's love when he could feel the milieu changing again. The buildings and the people were receding and fading away in the light. The pain incinerated his heart as Abhishek witnessed his mother's image waning away as well. He stretched out his hands in a desperate attempt to stop her but he was powerless. The gentle sepia hue of the sky was overtaken by a fiery red. Once again, the buildings and the crowd emerged in a rapid and haphazard manner but they looked dark and ominous. The contemporary view of Ganeshguri appeared again but it had a daunting visage. The crowd below swelled to infinite proportions and all eyes were fixed on him. The buildings continued growing till their tips pierced the heavens; they started to shake slowly as they came to life. Abhishek watched in horror as the crowd and the sentient concrete structures slowly marched towards him in a menacing manner. With each step they took, their numbers grew and so did their dimensions. Abhishek was rooted to his spot in fear as the swelling horde closed in. His muscles were frozen and they refused to budge, his eyes were spellbound like a moth caught in the gaze of light. He watched his impending doom arrive within striking distance. He was trapped on all sides and with each heartbeat his sense of despair grew stronger.

At that moment he felt the earth shake as he heard a distant voice calling him. The jolt grew stronger as he heard the same voice calling out his name. Abhishek was startled out of his trance and he turned around to find Pulakesh standing next to him. He felt the pressure release as Pulakesh's fingers pried away from his shoulder. He looked around him, everything was back to normal. There was no residue of the hostile crowd and the animate edifices, nor was there any trace of an older city. Gone too were images of his mother delicately trying to console him. Abhishek could not fathom if he was hallucinating or what he witnessed was for real. The images of his mother stayed with him for some time as he softly cried.

"Are you alright?" Pulakesh called him again. "I had been calling you for a long time but you were stupefied and gazing into the distance. Is everything okay?"

"I am doing fine, thanks for your concern. Why were you looking for me?"

"It's boss. He is back from the meeting with our client. He is asking for the work he had assigned to you. He wants to meet you right now."

Abhishek was shocked to know that he had been in a trance for nearly two hours, it felt like a few minutes to him.

"That old man does not like to be kept waiting. Come, let us proceed."

***

"So, Abhishek, are you done with your work?"

"No sir. I have not even started yet."

"I believe you have a good reason for your procrastination." Joseph's voice was colder than ice.

"I am battling some personal demons, sir. I need some time to complete the work assigned to me. I am not feeling well right now. I would be grateful to you if you will grant me leave for the day."

Like an enraged bull Joseph stepped towards Abhishek. His words came out through gritted teeth. "I am not going to do anything like that. You will stay here in office and in my presence, you will complete everything. I want to see how you spend your time in office. You will complete your task even if you have to stay here in this goddamned office till midnight. Is that understood?"

Abhishek stared blankly at his boss and expressed his views on the matter with two words. "Fuck Off."

Time had come to a standstill inside the tiny office in Guwahati. Nobody moved a muscle, nobody even drew a breath. Joseph did not know what hit him and he was too stunned to react. Pulakesh was caught in a mixture of awe and disbelief at the audacity of Abhishek and the rest were left gawking at the brazen show of defiance. It was the first time Abhishek made an attempt to rebel against the shackles of authority that sought to constrain him. He discovered that it was an emancipating experience. Life for him was already over; he had already suffered enough and did not have the patience to withstand the bickering of another entity who sought to impose his will upon him.

Without waiting for a reaction from Joseph and the rest, Abhishek stormed out of the building.

***

CHAPTER-11

A storm of hate which had been lying dormant inside Abhishek's psyche for a long time was now brewing up with a vengeance. Every fibre of his being was coursing with hate and anger against the world which had being so unjust to him. He wanted to lash out and hurt somebody, violence was playing in his mind and he needed an outlet. Without thinking Abhishek boarded an auto rickshaw. There was no planned destination in his mind, he simply told the driver to take him around Guwahati. If the driver was puzzled by the odd request he hid it well, his only concern was money.

Abhishek felt betrayed. His love for Piyushmita now morphed into vitriolic hate. He hated Amit even more for Abhishek believed that a guy like him was unworthy of the happiness that fate bestowed on his lap. Abhishek had never hurt anybody so why was he being unfairly punished? These thoughts tortured his mind. Abhishek spent the better part of the day crisscrossing through the streets of Guwahati, brooding in his thoughts of hate. When he finally stopped, it was late in the evening.

Abhishek had decided on his target, it would be Amit. Amit would have to pay the price for his deceit. Abhishek recalled the permanent address of his arch-enemy in Guwahati. Amit had shared it with him when they were friends and that day he decided to put that information to good use. Abhishek reached his destination and waited outside the gates. It was a beautiful house, well maintained and brightly illuminated. Both Amit and Piyushmita were in Delhi but Amit's old parents were in Guwahati. Abhishek decided to pay them a visit but stopped short, he was not adequately prepared for the mission. He promised himself to make the visit the next day.

The next day, Abhishek carried with him a jerry can of kerosene and also a lighter. His original intention was to use the kerosene for a far more diabolical purpose but even a man as consumed by rage as Abhishek shuddered at the thought and could not bring himself to carry it out. Instead he decided to leave a message for Amit.

Abhishek patiently waited for darkness to fall and the streets to get deserted. From his concealed position he saw a young lad, probably a house-help, lock the gates and retire inside. That was Abhishek's chance. He quickly emerged from hiding and emptied the can of kerosene on the wooden gates and the adjoining boundary fence. Without a moment's delay he lit the lighter and set the fuel on fire. The seething kerosene ignited instantly and the entrance was engulfed in flames. The fire did not quench his hate. Abhishek picked up stones lying by the street and hurled them at the house while mouthing expletives for Amit. He was so engrossed in his act that he failed to hear the screams emerging from the house, and the neighbours who gathered on the street.

Alarmed by the cries of help, the neighbours had showed up to aid the aggrieved family. What they discovered was a youth screaming obscenities and hurling stones at the house. Without wasting time, they gathered whatever weapons they could get and charged at Abhishek. The roar of so many people charging at him distracted Abhishek from his stupor and he panicked. Leaving all thoughts of vengeance behind him he fled for his life.

The crowd was relentless in their pursuit. One man in particular was determined to teach him a lesson. As Abhishek negotiated a blind turn on the street the man closed the distance and managed to land a strike on his shoulder. Abhishek winced from the blow; he lost balance and crashed on the street. The man bowed down to haul Abhishek who managed to get his hands on a loose brick and smashed it hard against his assailant's temple. The brick broke in two and the man collapsed to the ground without a sound. Abhishek had only a second to gather his thoughts. Horrified by what he had just done he started to run. He kept on running until he reached the main road and was lost in the milieu.

***

On reaching the safety of his home at Silpukhuri Abhishek locked himself inside his room. His body was trembling with fright and he felt like his heart would burst out of his chest any moment.

A wave of horror washed over Abhishek. His thoughts of hate were now replaced by the burden of guilt. He was shocked that he could descend so low. Abhishek always fancied himself as a gentle soul who could never hurt a living being. But what he displayed outside Amit's house was a barbaric act carried out by a blood-thirsty savage. Abhishek shuddered at the thought of the man he fought with on the street. The latter had collapsed without a sound and his body made no movement. Abhishek was scared and he huddled himself into a corner and wept. All he wanted was to rebel against the confinements placed on him by destiny, he wanted to take control and all he did was turn into a monster.

Fear numbed his senses and Abhishek discovered he was murmuring his thoughts aloud. The fear of an irate posse of police crashing through the door and dragging him away by the scruff of his neck possessed him. He was getting paranoid and the slightest noise would make his heart leap to his mouth. If he continued like that, he would go insane. To pacify his agitated mind Abhishek needed to calm down. It was impossible for him to maintain composure at his present condition so he decided to engage in some form of activity to rid his mind from all fears.

Abhishek turned his focus on the perpetually incomplete painting he had been working on. He picked up his satchel of brush and colours and took on the incomplete painting with a fanatical fervour. With every stroke of his brush he invoked the Gods and prayed for salvation. His hands worked tirelessly but his mind remained blank. There was no creativity or pleasure in his work. His mind was not free and his hands were gripped by fear. Try as much as he wanted, Abhishek could not give any shape on the canvas nor could he assuage his paranoia.

Frustrated with his failure to make a breakthrough Abhishek grew more restless in his approach. He would dab his brush with multiple colours and scrape it across the canvas only to be greeted with the sight of an unearthly hue. He tried to improve by repeating the process all over again but the results were still the same. He abandoned the brush and used his hands to spread the colour on the canvas but even such measures failed to yield fruit.

Minutes changed to hours and time flew away unchecked. His paranoia was now replaced by an obsession about the painting he had been trying to make for days. There was an occasional throbbing sound inside his head but Abhishek ignored it. His vision blurred and the throbbing sound in his head kept repeating with alarming regularity. He found it increasingly difficult to focus and even his legs were wavering but nonetheless he carried on. A flurry of shadows caught Abhishek's eye and he momentarily stopped to investigate the cause of the disturbance. He looked up at the wall facing him and he discovered that a moth was hopelessly attracted to the light of the incandescent bulb glowing softly. The moth was blissfully unaware of the cobweb gnarled around the font of light and the spider silently waiting in the lurch. The moth flapped away its tiny wings in front of the bulb casting oblique shadows over the room. More than once the moth was trapped in the web but it managed to wriggle out just in time. It was aware of the lurking danger around but also trapped in its own helpless awe of the shining light. The moth flew in a tight semi-circle and once again crashed into the web. But that time it had gone too far and there was no escape. The spider that was patiently waiting for its prey pounced upon it in a flash. Now it was just a matter of time before the moth's life was sucked out of it.

The scene disturbed Abhishek for more reasons than one and he could feel the fear growing stronger inside him. His limbs went stiff from the non-stop exertion but he did not dare give up. There was nothing left to apply on the canvas so Abhishek switched to the bottle of ink that was on the study table. He uncorked the bottle and in one swift motion, swung his arm at the canvas spilling ink all over the place. He continued with the practice until he ran out of ink. He had run out of materials but the painting was still not complete, what stood in front of him was a dark and repulsive image unfit for human evaluation.

With a cry of anguish, Abhishek reached for the penknife in his satchel and slashed his fingers. Blood was oozing uninhibitedly from his wounds but he was unperturbed. In a mad rush he scrambled his bloodied fingers over the mud of colours. Red stripes of blood merged with his dark creation producing something even more sinister. Abhishek continued scrambling his fingers in frenzy, his wounds awash with blood. The throbbing sound in his head that he heard at regular intervals had morphed into one long unceasing noise and he thought he could even hear human voices, but he could not stop.

In his zeal, his fingers pierced through the canvas but he was unrelenting in his efforts. Before he realized what was happening, his painting was in tatters. It was torn, shredded and pouring out blood, black and ruin. With an agonizing yell Abhishek fell on his knees, clutching his head in despair.

He had no idea for how long he was latching on to that position. The throbbing sound in his head grew louder and implacable with each passing moment until he felt his head would burst open. The human voice that accompanied the throbbing sound was also becoming coherent. He thought he could recognize the voice and realized that he in fact did recognize the voice, it was his father. What he thought were phantom voices in his head was his father banging on the door of his room.

"Abhishek! Abhishek open up. For the love of God please open the door."

Dreary eyed, Abhishek managed to drag himself to the door and unlock it. His father Arindam Baruah was standing at the door with his hands rigid and shoulders tense. Stress, panic, anger, concern and a myriad of other emotions were writ large on his father's face.

The old man gasped when his son opened the door. A gruesome sight greeted him. Standing in front of him was a person he could barely recognize. Clothed in muddied formals his son was washed in a multitude of colours, ink and grime. The colours on his body did not evoke any sense of revelry but that of pain and suffering. Abhishek's body was pale and emaciated. His eyes were red and sunk in its sockets because of fatigue, and there were dark circles underneath. The whole room was a mess and a foul odour was emitting from inside. The room was poorly lit but the old man could make out the litter strewn all over the place. The floor and the walls were disfigured which evoked a sense of hideousness and chaos. There was a mutilated canvas hanging on a stand in the middle of the room. Arindam couldn't believe it could support any art but colours of black, blue and red were dripping from the shredded remains.

"My God! It is blood dripping from your fingers, I thought it was paint. What have you been doing inside your room Abhishek?!"

"You don't have to shout." Abhishek replied in a tired voice. "I am tired and busy. Leave me alone."

"But ... but you have been inside there for so long!"

"Just go away and leave me in peace."

"You have been locked inside your room for three days. You have not eaten anything nor have you come out of your room. I was worried."

"Please leave me alone for the moment. I need some rest."

"You have been alone long enough. Come out, clean yourself and have some food. If need be I will call a doctor. And, also you need to bandage your wounds before..."
"I am not a child and I hate it when you treat me like one. I told you to leave so just leave." Abhishek barked.

"You don't know how much you scared me. If I am saying something then it is for your own good. I was so worried about you. If you did not open the door today, I would have burnt it down."

"Burning down things come very easily to you, don't they?" It was a cold accusation from Abhishek deliberately targeted at his father.

"Wha...What?" Arindam was taken aback.

"You know what I am talking about."

Arindam recoiled at the words. Like his son, Arindam too was fighting to bury the past and move on.

"I thought..."

"The problem with you is that you believe only you have the right to think. And you think only you are right, everybody else is wrong. You have neither patience nor tolerance for others' views. Only you have the right to take decisions in the family and the rest must follow. We had to live by your rules or face the consequences. For your headstrong attitude we all had to suffer. Things have changed too much; you should have known that by now. Some relations were burnt long ago and *you* are the one who lit the match."

Life was drained out of Arindam's face as he heard his son incriminate against him. The reasonably amiable behaviour from Abhishek in the past few days had given him hope that a burdened past could be unloaded. But the fresh allegations levelled against him reopened old wounds. Arindam cringed at the words flung at him, more so because he knew there was some truth in what had been said. For years he regretted his temperamental past and tried to make amends, but a silent barrier between him and his son prevented any reconciliation. And before he realized, the rift between father and son had gone too wide. There were times when he wished he could have been moderate in his behaviour but it was to no avail. What had been hurt could not be healed and the constant pain that had accompanied the family would linger on.

"I... I am sorry." The words were spoken very softly, barely a whisper. But it carried the weight of years of guilt pending inside him. He hoped the voice would reach out to his son.

"It is too late for that." Abhishek replied in an equally soft tone. No further words were exchanged but none was required. Their silence had said it all. Abhishek retired to his room and locked up the door behind him.

***

CHAPTER-12

The month of October was approaching its final days and autumn had steadily swept in. The meteorologists predicted an unusually harsh winter. The early chill and withered, falling leaves of the trees were a testimony to their claim. But October was also the month of joy and festivities. Durga Puja is one of the biggest festivals in Assam and held in a grand manner every year in the state. The sea of people that come to witness and take part in the festivities was an ever-lasting symbol for the zest of life.

Celebrations came early to the Guwahati branch of *Creations* as one lucrative deal after another was signed under the auspices of the new branch head Pulakesh. Joseph praised the boy to high heavens and predicted a bright future for him in the industry.

Happiness also paid a visit to the lives of Amit and Piyushmita during the season. Amit was beside himself with grief when he had heard about the act of arson committed at his Guwahati residence. But his concerns were allayed when his mother informed him that nobody was injured in the act and the damage done would be repaired within days. The only matter of concern was for their neighbour Mr. Sharma who chased after the perpetrator and was injured in the melee. He was lying unconscious on the street and had to be hospitalized. He has been in coma since.

The culprit could not be apprehended by the public or the police but his mother advised Amit to forget the incident as a bad dream. There were happier things to focus on. Amit and Piyushmita had informed their respective families about their relationship and they would be taking things forward in their forthcoming visit to Guwahati during Puja celebrations.

***

The only house bereft of joy during the Puja festivities was located on the hills of Navagraha in Silpukhuri. The lonely house was silhouetted in a sea of light that engulfed it. There were only two occupants in the house. They both were strangers to each other and neither had any contact with the rest of society. Arindam Baruah, the senior occupant of the house was a broken man. His only child Abhishek was reduced to a wreck and he was helpless to do anything about it.

Relationship between the father and the son had always been under strain. But deep inside him Arindam nurtured a wishful dream that he could alter the past and make things better again. For a brief moment, it looked like his dreams would come true but then the world around him came crashing down.

Arindam harboured no illusions about his role as a father. He had been a terrible parent and a horrible family man. He was aware of his shortcomings, of his impulsive temper and instinct for violence. But no matter how much he tried, the monster inside his soul always overpowered him.

Arindam pondered over the root cause of his troubles. It did not take him long to realize that the answers lied in his own troubled past. He had a hard childhood. At a time of grave crisis, he was abandoned by his dear and loved ones. Nobody extended a loving hand or a word of consolation in his personal loss. Arindam was left alone to fend for himself in an unkind world. He subsequently lost faith in human relations and viewed emotions as a sign of weakness. He grew up in extreme hardship, getting acquainted with hunger and poverty along the way. At an age when children would play and make merry he had to do odd jobs to survive. He had to fight every step of his life, often in the literal sense. Over the years he was feared and respected in the neighbourhood as a hard man.

His perseverance bore fruit and he triumphed over adversity. He had managed to educate himself and find a job. But victory had come at a cost. Arindam had honed himself as a tough and aggressive individual, attributes which would later cause havoc in his own family.

A mercurial temper honed by years of aggression became an inseparable part of Arindam's persona. He was a no-nonsense man and had little patience with people who could not match up to his standards. His family had to bear the brunt of his fury which would erupt anytime and at the slightest of provocations. His own family feared him. It was not a conscious decision on Arindam's part to intimidate them but bitterness was so deeply etched in his mind that he was unable to restrain himself. He had seen fear, and even hate, in the eyes of Abhishek when there should have been love.

Tears welled up in Arindam's eyes as painful memories resurged. Countless times he had berated himself for his hostile attitude, he wanted to change and become a softer person; yet countless times he had failed. The violent showdowns with his family would continue unabated until everything was lost. He no longer lived with his son but with a stranger who would rarely speak to him and had very little in common.

It crushed Arindam that his son Abhishek had to pay the price for his actions as a father. Abhishek grew up with a scarred childhood, intimidated of the people around him. The little boy refused to leave the house because his friends taunted him on the playground. Strangers would stop him on the road and deliberately ask him uncomfortable questions about his family, deriving a sadistic pleasure from the young boy's obvious distress. As a result, Abhishek severed ties with the outside world and withdrew into a shell.

Arindam recalled his son's fear of going to school. Abhishek would often cry and complain of being bullied in the class by other students. Being a loner, he had no friends and everybody would pick on him as an easy target. As a father, Arindam should have addressed the problems, instead he chided his son for being a weak coward. His son endured school life by his own means.

It was when Arindam left for Delhi that the burden of solitude weighed upon Arindam's shoulders. Loneliness was a disease that many experienced but few were able to comprehend, and both father and son were ailing from it. Arindam did not care to know the whereabouts of his son in Delhi or what he was doing there. For ten years there was no communication between the two. But the confinement of a deserted house was eating into the soul of Arindam.

With great effort he had mustered the courage to speak to his son over the phone. He would talk about mundane and even irrelevant things, anything so that he could at least hear his son's voice. But that did little to mitigate his sense of isolated existence. Finding no other recourse, Arindam deliberately spoke lies to his son about his failing health. He would never know whether it was sympathy or some other reason but his son did come back to him.

Arindam hoped that things would improve after his son's arrival but it was a futile hope. There was indifference in Abhishek's attitude towards his father. Yet there was also an absence of belligerence which spawned hope in Arindam. But the silent barrier between them which had evolved over the years was not easy to break down.

Things gradually took a turn for the worse. Abhishek would leave house early in the morning and return late at night. As a father, Arindam was concerned but he did not dare to express his concerns in front of his son for the fear of ridicule. At first, he did not notice, but later Arindam realized his son was fighting over a lot of issues. Often Abhishek would suffer from hallucinations; he would live in his own imaginary world and make imaginary friends. More than once Arindam caught his son speaking animatedly to himself. For Abhishek, the barrier between reality and imagination was fast dissolving.

One night, Abhishek had returned home late at night in a harried state. He was screaming in terror and locked himself in the room. The father in Arindam could not watch any longer and he immediately rushed to his son's aid. For three days Arindam kept banging on the door of his son's room but Abhishek refused to heed to his father's call. When the door opened Arindam could not recognize his own son. As a father he tried to reconcile but Abhishek had severed all familial relations like Arindam himself once did.

Since that day Abhishek would mostly confine himself to his room, suffering from paranoia and refusing to leave the house even once. Arindam had no idea what was ailing his son, but he prayed to the Gods that they rid Abhishek off his misery. As a distraught father that was the only thing he could do. The world he had tried to build was shattered and Arindam would have to live alone among the broken pieces.

***

Abhishek had irrevocably withdrawn into a shell shunning all contacts with the world outside. He tried everything possible by him to reconstruct his life but all his efforts were laid to waste. His hopes, dreams and aspirations were all blown up in smoke. There was nothing left for Abhishek but to accept the inevitable.

The condition of his room mirrored the sorry state of his life. It was untidy, gloomy and chaotic with scant respect for belongings which were strewn everywhere. A disfigured canvas that was left incomplete stood silent guard over the debris. A broken clay elephant, a gift for him from Amit, was lying undisturbed at its feet. A whiff of tobacco smoke hung in the air dispersing its burnt odour across the room. By some miracle the smoke survived even after the cigarettes were long burnt out, but every passing day the smoke was slowly and gradually fading away.

Abhishek's memory was steadily failing him. He no longer had any recollection of his past but he believed that once upon a time even he was happy. The gentle touch of his mother and her soothing words as he remembered were the only memories left with him.

For years Abhishek had hated himself and the world around him.

But he no longer held a grudge against anyone. There was nothing left of the hate, only a yearning for peace. His sense of attachment and desires has long been vanquished. He was alone and tired and all he wished for was to rest in peace.

Abhishek developed a more sympathetic view of his father whom he had previously judged with raw prejudice. His old man was also a victim of circumstances and a puppet in the hands of destiny. He was conscious of the efforts his father made to reconcile with him; in all honesty he wanted the same. But too much time had transpired between them to correct the mistakes of the past.

From the window in his room Abhishek could make the faint outline of the Navagraha Temple in the distance. Night had descended and a canopy of stars adored the temple. The stars were burning brightly and some of them seemed to sing a symphony of their own. It was the occasion of Durga Puja and sitting in his room Abhishek could hear the drums beating on the street. Durga Puja is commemorated to honour the killing of the demon Mahisasura by Goddess Durga. Abhishek could feel his own inner demons finally laid to rest. There was nothing more he could ask for from the Gods.

The dream-catcher dangled lifelessly over his bed.

Abhishek felt a chill in the air and he could sense that winter was just around the corner. It was autumn and the last leaf of the solitary *Krishnasura* tree was falling to the ground.

THE END

www.ingramcontent.com/pod-product-compliance
Lightning Source LLC
Chambersburg PA
CBHW021926170626
46807CB00007B/3007